All of Alessia

by

Saraphina Heart

"It wasn't his hands that undressed her.
It was the way he looked at her."

Aquilar Publishing
Connecticut, USA

ISBN: 978-1-969097-29-4

This book was written and created entirely by a human author. No generative artificial intelligence was used in the writing, editing, or design of this work.

Printed in the United States of America

Prelude

The Dream

She saw him from across the room.

The soft hum of conversation, the clinking of glasses, and an amber glow of light surrounded all her senses. Her breath caught... not because of how he looked, though he was striking in a quiet and strong way, but because of how he made her feel.

Seen.

Even as he laughed politely with someone else, his gaze kept drifting back to her. Each stolen glance was a secret message; one she felt beneath her skin. She tried to focus on the conversation in front of her, nodding, smiling, pretending; but something had stirred. Something she had only heard and read about.

Later, they found each other at the bar. As if it was planned.

"Do you remember me?" he asked, voice low and smooth like velvet over stone.

She blinked, the question echoing in her chest. "I think... we met once. A long time ago."

A slow smile played at his lips. "I remember."

They talked. About nothing and everything. About the way bourbon bites and how the rain had just begun to fall outside.

He brushed her arm once... twice, and each time her skin burned in the best way. She leaned in closer, not entirely by choice, but because her body needed to.

The kiss came later. Deep. Hungry. Beautiful.

It was the kind of kiss that silenced doubt and woke desire. She melted into him, into the feeling she didn't realize she'd been

aching for. A connection not just of lips, but of something more essential. Something broken inside her trying to be whole again.

And when they met again, the very next night, for dinner... that spark ignited into fire. No pretense. No games. Just hands, breath, and need.

Their hands found each other first. Fingers grazing skin with tentative curiosity, then with purpose. As if they'd done this before in another life. As if their bodies were only waiting for this moment to remember.

They didn't make it past the hallway.

Pressed against the wall, her breath caught again... not from surprise, but from recognition. His mouth moved to her neck, slow, reverent, tracing the pulse that betrayed her longing. She tilted her head, offering more.

He murmured her name again, like he'd always known how to say it.

Clothes slipped away without urgency, like falling petals. Her back met cool sheets. Then warmth. Then him.

His hands were a heated caress against her soft skin, awakening something deep and forbidden. The desire pulsed through her like something illicit, almost dangerous, but completely hers.

She arched into him as his lips found hers again, then her neck, then lower.

His mouth and tongue were both hard and soft on her breasts, igniting waves of sensation. Her breath turned to gasps, her body aching for more as his mouth followed the path of his hand, moving lower.

He paused.

His hand slipped between her thighs... gentle, sure, knowing.

Every stroke sent sparks ricocheting through her spine. She moaned, barely able to breathe, every nerve lit.

Then his mouth replaced his hand.

It wasn't just pleasure, it was possession. Worship. His mouth became more than magic, it became part of her. She cried out, hands tangled in his hair, body trembling with the intensity of it all.

And when she couldn't take it anymore, she pulled him up to her, whispering his name like a plea.

He entered her in one slow, perfect movement.

It was as if they were one.

He filled her completely. His size, his warmth, his skin... it was all perfect. They moved together in rhythm, her body rising to meet his in waves of passion. Fast. Slow. Fast again.

They built a rhythm together, primal and beautiful, her body no longer her own, and his name the only word she could form.

She clung to him, nails at his shoulders, as pleasure built inside her like a storm ready to break.

He whispered her name like a prayer.

And when the end came, it came for both of them... together.

Raw. Honest. Divine.

⊡

She woke up, flushed and tangled in the sheets, the dream still wrapped around her like silk. Her body throbbed, but it was her soul that felt raw and alive.

She pressed a hand to her lips, still tasting him. Still feeling everything.

This time, she wouldn't just dream it.

This time, she would find it.

Chapter 1

The Awakening

The sun filtered through the blinds, casting soft lines across her bare legs. She blinked, heart still racing from the dream. The sheets clung to her skin like memory.

Mmmmmmm.

She pressed her thighs together, as if she could hold onto the sensation just a little longer, knowing she wanted more. It was just a dream and she knew that. But it felt more real than anything she'd touched in a long time.

In the silence of her apartment, the contrast hit hard. No voice calling her name. No fingers tracing fire across her skin.

Just the tick of the clock and the hum of the fridge.

She rose, wrapped a robe around her naked body, and glided to the kitchen. Her body still buzzed, but it was the ache beneath the desire that lingered most. The part of her that had been shut down for too long. Closed. Guarded.

Not by choice.

She'd lived alone for years now. Long enough to know exactly how she liked things... everything had its place, its rhythm.

That was the control she could manage when the world outside had so often felt out of reach.

Predictable routines. Clean counters. Soft music and a candle by the bed. There was comfort in that.

Control had been her armor.

The reasons for it were stacked like files in the back of her mind. Relationships that fizzled. Lies and loss. Moments where

"no" hadn't been enough. Years of playing small to feel safe.

She wasn't broken but she had learned to build walls.

Her therapist had once called it protective numbness, and warned her she'd have to tear it down brick by brick. It helped her survive. But now... she was starting to want more than survival. She wanted to feel. To burn.

She had taken the time to know herself. To understand what she wanted, not just in a man but in life. In her body. In her spirit.

And that dream... that impossible, wild, beautiful dream had lit something she hadn't realized was still alive.

She poured her coffee and stared out the window.

What if I stopped holding back?

What if I found something, or someone, that made me feel like that dream again?

Someone who lets me be me. Someone I could explore with.

Her hand tightened around the mug. Not in fear.

In decision.

Chapter 2

Becoming Her

She stood in front of the mirror, watching as the stylist fluffed her long curls into place.

It had been too long since she let someone else touch her hair.

Too long since she looked in the mirror and saw not just a face, but a woman.

A beautiful one.

She left the salon with her head a little higher, her stride a little slower, a sultry sway to her hips. She felt eyes on her and, for once, she didn't shrink beneath them.

She stopped by a boutique on impulse. The kind of place she usually passed without a second glance. Today, something pulled her in.

The silk bra she chose was deep wine... dark, rich, and seductive. The panties, lacy and delicate, hugged all the right curves. She held the set against herself in the dressing room and smiled.

She thought it wasn't for anyone else. Just her. But she was very wrong.

She changed into a soft, fitted dress that clung to her body like it knew her secrets. Slipped on heels. Light perfume. Lip gloss.

Her reflection was familiar and new all at once. She didn't allow herself to be beautiful before, but now she was ready to shine.

As she stepped outside, the city felt different. Brighter. Her heels clicked confidently on the sidewalk, her hips swaying to a rhythm only she could hear.

And then... he was there.

Or something like him.

Not in form, but in sensation.

She passed a man whose scent reminded her of the man in her dream. Just a trace of it, but it hit her like a flame to dry paper.

Her breath caught. Her body remembered what it had never truly known.

His skin against mine.

His strong body between my legs.

Oh damn...

She shook her head, cheeks flushed, a smile pulling at her lips.

Her mind was getting away from her.

But wasn't that the point?

She was beginning to feel beautiful again. Powerful. Alive.

She didn't need permission to feel those things. She didn't need a dream to justify them.

She was becoming the woman she dreamed of being.

Chapter 3

The Encounter

She turned the corner, lost in thought and the echo of his imagined touch... when she saw him.

Not a memory. Not a fantasy.

Him.

Standing just feet away, as real as the street beneath her heels.

Tall. Confident. That same quiet strength. The same eyes that undressed her with a glance in her dream.

She couldn't believe her eyes. She blinked, wondering if it was a dream. But then he looked up and locked eyes with her.

Her breath hitched. Heat surged to her cheeks. Her skin prickled with awareness, every nerve humming like it already knew what came next. For a heartbeat, the world spun just slightly off its axis.

Did he feel it too?

Was it possible?

Could he have dreamed it too?

He smiled... slow, familiar, devastating.

"I'm sorry," he said, tilting his head with that same velvet-rich voice, "but do I know you?"

She opened her mouth. Closed it. Her heart slammed against her ribs.

Say something. Anything.

"I... I think maybe..." she stammered, swallowing hard. "We might've... met before?" It came out a question.

His smile widened just slightly. "Maybe in a dream?"

Her knees nearly buckled. Could he know?

Could he somehow see the image in her mind... his body pressed against hers, his hands everywhere, her name on his lips?

She was flushed, pulsing, alive. Wanting him to take her right there, against the wall of the café behind them, or the alley beside them, or just—

He extended his hand. "I'm Leander."

She blinked. "I'm..." Who was she again?

She shook herself. "Alessia," she managed. "I'm Alessia."

She wanted, needed, to hear her name pass slowly over his lips.

His fingers wrapped around hers—warm, strong, steady—and the moment they touched, it was all there again.

Those hands... What those hands could do to her.

The fire. The possibility.

Chapter 4

The Rain, the Heat

The next morning, Alessia stepped out for coffee, dressed to the nines. Her heels clicked rhythmically on the sidewalk, each step exuding confidence. She felt the eyes on her... the way her dress hugged her curves, the way her long hair fell across her bare back, the way her waist moved with her hips. She felt powerful. Desirable. Whole.

And then she saw him. Leander.

Her mind went there instantly... the dream, the fire, the way he touched her, filled her.

They locked eyes. His lips curled into a slow smile, and without hesitation, he stood. They left the café together, walking side by side down a quiet street, the easy rhythm between them filling the space with energy.

They talked like they had always known each other. But when the clouds opened and rain began to fall, he took her hand without a word and led her quickly down the block.

She barely noticed where they were going. Just the feeling of his fingers wrapped around hers. Until—

This looks familiar...

They made their way up to his penthouse, the door clicking closed behind them. He showed her to the bathroom and offered her a towel through the cracked door. It was warm.

Fresh. Thoughtful.

She took a breath, pressed it to her damp skin, and paused.

When she emerged, he was waiting in the living room, wearing a loosely tied robe. She couldn't look away.

She walked to him, her towel wrapped tightly around her. The space between them was thick with the unspoken.

He stepped closer.

She felt his breath on her lips. Then his mouth met hers... hungry, sure, and completely familiar.

Her hand rested on his thigh, and she felt the warmth of his skin beneath the robe. His fingers slipped beneath the edge of her towel, resting gently on her leg, then climbing higher.

She moved her hand, found the opening in his robe, and slid her fingers inside, upward but tentative at first. Curious.

Starved.

His fingers explored her slowly, parting her gently. Her breath caught. She was already wet and aching. When his finger found that sensitive spot at the center of her, she whimpered, unable to hold back.

"Shall we go upstairs?" he asked, lips brushing hers.

She nodded. "Yes."

They moved together up the stairs. She undressed under his hands. He undressed beneath hers. When he entered her, it was slow. Deep. Real.

Together, they didn't just make love. They became it.

Chapter 5

The Morning After

Sunlight poured through the linen curtains. Alessia stirred, slowly opening her eyes to the warmth of the room and the warmth of him.

Leander lay beside her, one arm beneath her neck, the other resting across her bare waist. His breathing was steady, deep.

Peaceful.

She took a moment to simply feel... no guilt. No fear. Just calm.

When he stirred, his voice was still laced with sleep.

"Morning."

She smiled. "Morning."

He leaned in and kissed her temple. "I'll make coffee."

She changed into her dress from the night before, touched up her gloss, and slipped her heels back on. She looked in the hallway mirror and saw not a woman leaving someone's bed, but a woman walking boldly into her life.

At the door, he asked, "Will I see you again?"

She smiled. "You will."

Chapter 6

Noticed

Alessia stepped into the office just after nine, fresh from a quiet cab ride, a new energy coiled inside her like a secret.

Heads turned.

It wasn't just her dress, though the soft blush silk fell just right, or the sleek way her hair was pulled back with loose tendrils framing her face.

It was her.

She radiated something new. Something untouchable.

"Morning, Alessia," her coworker Sam said, blinking. "You look... incredible."

She smiled. "Thank you."

When her friend Lila leaned in at lunch and whispered, "Okay, what's going on with you?" Alessia simply sipped her coffee and said, "Nothing. Everything."

Later that afternoon, the receptionist called out, "There's something for you."

A black gift box waited on her desk, elegant and sleek, tied with a deep red satin ribbon.

No card. No label.

She opened it slowly.

Inside, resting on black velvet, was a red eye mask. Not cliché.

Not cheap.

Intricate. Crocheted. Sensual. Designed to be felt as much as worn.

She lifted it, and beneath it was a folded piece of handmade paper.

"For the next time you close your eyes and let go. It's not about what I see when you wear it...

It's about what you feel when you can't see, because your other senses take over.

—L"

Her breath caught.

This wasn't just flirtation.

It was an invitation.

A promise.

Chapter 7
The Reply

That evening, Alessia didn't panic. She didn't overanalyze.

She lit not one candle...but three.

She stepped into the shower, steam curling around her, and let the water pour over her back, her breasts, her thighs... each drop waking her skin again, reminding her of where his hands had been.

A soft gasp escaped her lips.

Then, slowly, she let her hands glide lower.

She felt herself. Truly felt. Her pulse throbbed. Her body vibrated with new awareness.

She reached for the shower wand. The water pulsed at her neck, then her breast and her nipple responded instantly. She moved it lower, to the place his mouth had been.

She gasped again.

She didn't know she could feel like this. Didn't know she could want like this.

Wrapped in a towel, glowing from within, she reached for her phone.

Alessia:

I think I'm ready to let go.

But I hope you're ready for what you asked for...

(She attached a photo of her face partially obscured by the mask, a hint of smile on her lips, her hair loose and wild.)

Send.

Minutes later, while brushing her hair, her phone lit up.

Leander:

That photo is burned into me.

You have no idea how hard I'm trying not to come to you right now.

But I will wait.

Because next time... you won't just be wearing the mask.

You'll be begging to keep it on.

—L

She nearly dropped the phone. Her knees threatened to give way.

She stood in silence, one hand gripping the counter.

It wasn't just what he said, it was what he saw in her.

Chapter 8

The Answer

She lay in bed, freshly moisturized, scented, bare beneath the covers.

She slept soundly.

Peacefully.

Not because someone had touched her but because she had finally touched her soul.

When morning came, light warm against her cheek, she reached for her phone.

Alessia:

Tell me when.

Tell me where.

I'll bring the mask.

Send.

Chapter 9

A New Rhythm

She didn't need to rush. Not tonight.

She would become the woman he already saw.

She began by massaging warm, scented oil gently between her thighs, smoothing it into the delicate folds of skin where she knew his breath would hover.

She scooped a sweet cream and circled it over her nipples, watching them tighten beneath her touch. For him to taste.

She dabbed perfume behind her ears. At her throat. Lower still, where only he would find it.

Her lips were painted next... deep red, inviting, sinful.

Then she paused.

Is this okay?

Is it okay to want this much? To prepare like this? To crave and to control and to seduce?

Her chest tightened.

What would he think?

What would the world think?

She looked in the mirror.

And then, softly:

"This is who I am."

"I want this."

"That doesn't make me shameful."

"That makes me honest."

She stood taller.

She smiled.

And she picked up the mask.

Chapter 10

The Invitation

Her phone buzzed.

It was still early. The sun had barely warmed her windowsill.

Alessia rolled onto her side, the sheet falling from her bare shoulder, and blinked down at the screen.

Leander:

Tonight.

8 PM.

My place.

Wear something that makes you feel like a secret.

Bring the mask.

You won't need anything else.

Come alone. Come ready.

The door will be unlocked.

When you enter, I want you to put the mask on.

And wait for me in silence.

She stared at the message, her thumb hovering just above it.

Her mouth parted. A shiver trailed down her spine.

It was precise.

It was firm.

It was hot.

But more than that, it was an extension of trust. He was asking her to meet him not just physically, but emotionally. To give over control... and find freedom in it.

She closed her eyes.

And smiled.

Chapter 11

The Day Between

The day moved slowly.

Too slowly.

Alessia tried to focus... on emails, on meetings, on mundane decisions like oat milk or almond in her coffee. But every task felt like noise beneath the hum of something louder, deeper.

8 PM.

His place.

Wear something that makes you feel like a secret.

The words repeated in her mind like a pulse.

She sat in a strategy meeting with her team, nodding at slides, clicking through numbers... but her mind kept slipping.

To his voice.

To his hands.

To the idea of standing in his entryway, masked, silent, exposed.

She felt a warm rush spread between her thighs just thinking about it.

When she excused herself to the restroom, she leaned over the sink and stared at her reflection. Her skin was flushed, her pupils dilated.

She looked aroused. And afraid. And ready.

Is it too much? Am I too much?

What if he opens that door and sees more than I'm ready to show?

But another voice rose beneath the fear, the one she was learning to trust.

What if he already sees you... and still wants more?

By lunch, she stopped pretending to be fine.

She took a half day.

At home, she paced in her bedroom, pulling open drawers, rifling through delicate lace and silk. She held up piece after piece.

Too obvious.

Too aggressive.

Too... not her.

Then she found it.

A black slip of sheer chiffon... thin, barely-there straps, a whisper of coverage, the color of ink and night. It flowed like breath but clung like intention.

She tried it on and stood in front of the mirror.

It was perfect. She was perfect.

Mysterious. Sensual. A secret, just as he'd asked.

She packed the mask gently into a black clutch, painted her lips a deep plum, and dabbed perfume low on her throat.

It was only 5:00.

Three more hours.

She'd never felt this alive waiting for anything in her life.

Chapter 12

The Arrival

By 7:54 PM, Alessia was parked just a few doors down from

Leander's townhouse.

She hadn't meant to arrive early.

But she couldn't bear to be late.

Her fingers drummed the leather steering wheel. Her heart beat steady, but heavy. A slow, rhythmic thunder in her chest.

She glanced down at herself once more. The black slip hugged her curves like second skin, hidden beneath a long coat. Her lips were dark, inviting. The mask rested beside her in the passenger seat, its red lace glowing like embers under the streetlight.

She didn't touch it yet.

Not until the door.

Not until she stepped over.

7:58.

She stepped out of the car, heels clicking on the quiet pavement. The air was cool, brushing her bare legs beneath her coat. The neighborhood was still. No one watching.

Her eyes locked on his front door.

Dark wood. No light on the porch. No sound from within.

Just the promise.

She climbed the steps.

Her pulse quickened.

One breath in.

Another out.

She reached for the doorknob.

Unlocked.

She stepped inside.

The warmth hit her first. The faint scent of sandalwood.

Candles flickered somewhere deeper in the house.

She closed the door behind her and stood in silence.

Then, slowly, deliberately, she pulled the mask from her clutch and tied it behind her head.

The fabric pressed soft against her skin, the lace teasing her vision.

She slipped off her coat and let it fall to the floor.

She was alone.

Waiting.

Listening.

Bare but for the slip and the mask. Standing in his space, his light, his silence.

Her breath was the only sound in the room.

And then...

A soft click.

Footsteps on hardwood.

Closer. And closer.

Chapter 13

I Want It All

She stood in stillness.

The mask filtered the light, casting everything in red-hued shadow. Her breath was soft and measured, but her heart was pounding.

Then a creak.

More Footsteps.

Slow. Deliberate. Coming closer.

Her anticipation rose with every step.

Each one echoed in her chest like a drumbeat.

He's coming. He's here.

She heard him before she felt him.

And then his breath. Warm, close. Near her ear, her cheek, her neck.

She shivered.

A gentle brush of fingertips grazed her upper arm, tracing the line from her shoulder to her elbow. She tensed. Not in fear but in need.

Then she felt his hand move through her hair, loosening the strands, letting them spill against her back. His fingers tangled gently at the base of her neck.

Another sensation, soft and ticklish, dragging along her opposite arm. A feather? A scarf? She couldn't tell.

Then, across her chest.

She gasped.

She opened her mouth to speak, to say his name and ask for more... but before the word could form, a single finger pressed gently to her lips.

Not yet.

The air thickened. Her knees weakened.

Then, his voice... low, smooth, just above a whisper.

“What do you want?”

She didn’t hesitate.

Didn’t flinch.

Didn’t pretend.

“I want it all.”

Chapter 14

Please

The room was silent.

Only the soft flicker of candlelight and the gentle rhythm of

Alessia's breath filled the space. The mask blurred her vision, but she could sense him.

Nearby.

Watching.

Waiting.

Her pulse pounded in her throat. She tried to stay still. Tried to obey.

But the silence wrapped tighter around her than the slip clinging to her skin.

She heard his steps. Measured. Barefoot on hardwood.

Then... nothing.

She felt him, not in touch, but in the air. Close. So close.

Her mouth parted.

Her body ached.

And before she could stop herself, the word slipped out.

"Please..."

It wasn't loud.

It wasn't desperate.

It was hungry.

A second passed.

Then a third.

His steps resumed, closer now, deliberate. She heard him exhale through his nose, low and warm.

He circled behind her. The heat of his body near her back. She felt the brush of his fingers at her neck, then the whisper of his lips beside her ear.

"You couldn't wait, could you?"

She shook her head. Just once. Not ashamed.

"Good," he murmured.

His hand moved into her hair, twisting gently at the nape, and he pulled just enough to tilt her chin upward.

"You followed the rules until you couldn't."

His fingers dragged down the center of her chest, feather-light.

"That's the moment I wanted."

She trembled. And this time, she let herself.

Chapter 15

In His Arms

His fingers stayed tangled in her hair, firm but careful. Her head tilted back, lips parted, breath trembling.

He kissed her neck.

Not once. Not quickly.

Slow. Intimate. Possessive.

His lips moved along her throat, tasting her pulse as it thundered beneath her skin. She gasped when his mouth found her jawline.

Her lips.

The kiss wasn't gentle. It wasn't teasing.

It was devouring.

His mouth took hers with hunger, with reverence. It was a kiss that said, I've waited for this... but also I will never be done with you.

She moaned softly into him, pressing closer, letting his hand in her hair guide the rhythm. Her whole body melted into the sensation. His tongue met hers, slow at first... then deep.

God, this kiss.

It wasn't like the ones in her dreams. It was better.

Real. Rooted. Right.

And in that moment, she knew.

She wanted all of it.

Not just the touch. Not just the dominance.

But him.

The connection. The burn. The feeling of being wanted and seen and taken in pieces.

She'd been through so much, closed so many doors and buried so many parts of herself just to survive. But now?

Was this what it felt like for other people?

Did everyone get to feel this? This depth? This hunger?

Was it luck? Fate? Did she, after everything, deserve this?

He broke the kiss only to lift her.

One arm beneath her knees. One beneath her back.

She didn't resist. Didn't speak. She just held on.

Her head fell gently against his shoulder. Her hands curled around his neck.

And as he carried her into the next room, she thought:

I could stay in his arms forever.

Chapter 16

Not Just Yet

He carried her like she was something precious.

And when he laid her down, it was with intention.

The room was dim, lit by only a few scattered candles, but

Alessia could feel his presence above her. The warmth of him.

The steadiness.

And then...

His lips.

Not on her mouth.

But at her temple.

Then beneath her ear, where her breath caught in her throat.

Down to her collarbone, where he paused, inhaled, and pressed his mouth softly like a vow.

She reached for him, on instinct, but he gently caught her hand and placed it back against the bed.

"No," he whispered. "Just let me."

And so she did.

His lips moved lower.

Across the soft curve of her breast, where he lingered, tongue teasing, until her nipple stood tight and needy. She moaned... soft, breathy. He moved lower.

A kiss on the curve of her hip.

Another on the inside of her thigh.

Her body tensed, waiting for the next, quite certain he'd go where she needed him most.

But instead?

He knelt, wrapped his hands gently around her calf... and placed a warm kiss on the back of her knee.

Then, lower still, to the top of her foot.

She laughed. Not from humor, but from disbelief. From want.

"You're torturing me," she whispered.

He rose again, eyes gleaming.

"I haven't even started," he murmured.

He reached to the nightstand and picked up a glass of water.

Took a sip. Then, without warning, dragged an ice cube across her lips, letting the melt drip into her mouth.

She gasped at the cold, and the surprise.

Then the cube traced down her neck. Over her collarbone.

Slowly. Excruciatingly. It slipped between her breasts, catching the sensitive dip between them.

She writhed.

The cube continued gliding over her belly, trailing a ribbon of wet heat.

Down her thigh. Around her hip.

Almost to where she needed him.

Then it circled up the other thigh. So close.

So frustratingly close.

She gasped again, this time sharp, desperate.

He paused, hovering just above the place she ached for him.

“Still cold?” he asked, voice low, lips near her ear.

She turned her face toward him, her mouth curving.

“No,” she whispered. “Just cruel.”

And they both laughed... soft, shared, breathless.

But beneath the laughter was fire.

And under the fire, something else:

Trust.

Chapter 17

Surrender

He set the glass down, ice melting slowly inside.

Alessia's body trembled with need... wet from water, and wet from want. She arched her hips toward him, silently begging for more.

His hand hovered.

He looked at her. Through the mask. Beneath the skin.

And finally, finally, he touched her.

His fingers slid gently between her thighs. Slow. Reverent. The barest pressure at first. Just enough for her to gasp and part her legs further.

"Yes," she whispered, breath trembling.

But his pace didn't change.

He circled her softly, spreading slick warmth over every sensitive inch.

It wasn't enough.

She reached for his wrist, tried to guide him. "Faster," she murmured, breath catching. "Please..."

He caught her hand again and kissed her knuckles.

"No."

His voice was steady. Kind. Unshakable.

"Not tonight."

He kissed the inside of her thigh, just above where his fingers worked her with aching slowness.

“I want you to feel it all. Every second. Every inch.”

He leaned in. “You deserve that.”

She whimpered, frustration and wonder tangled in her chest.

But then he pressed his thumb just right, and her body answered.

It wasn’t a rush. It was a slow climb. A warm flood building in waves.

She rocked against him, hands gripping the sheets. Her eyes fluttered behind the mask.

He moved over her like a current... never hurried, never unsure. He tasted her next, his tongue tender and confident, tracing her softly until she was a trembling mess beneath him.

She came slowly, completely, like a quiet storm that swelled from the inside out.

And even as her body relaxed, his didn’t stop.

He kissed her hips.

Her belly.

Her breast.

Then her lips, deep and lingering, like a question asked and answered all at once.

He laid beside her, body pressed to hers, hand brushing her jaw.

“Again?” he asked softly.

She smiled into his mouth.

"Yes," she whispered.

"But this time, I want to feel you inside me."

"Slow."

He nodded once, eyes dark with devotion.

And moved over her like worship.

Chapter 18

Afterglow

The room was quiet, thick with warmth and the scent of skin and candle wax.

Alessia lay still, her breath slowly returning to its rhythm. Her legs still trembled faintly. Her body hummed.

She felt his fingers first, light against the back of her head.

Then the soft tug of fabric as he loosened the mask's tie and slid it free.

Her eyes blinked in the dim light.

And then she saw him.

Leander. She really saw him.

His face was open, flushed, beautiful. There was no dominance now. No heat. Just care.

He brushed her cheek with the back of his hand and kissed her... tenderly, deeply, without urgency.

"Was it everything you wanted?" he asked against her lips.

"Anything you didn't enjoy?"

She shook her head slowly, smiling. "I've never felt like that before."

He raised an eyebrow. "Like what?"

"Like I belonged to my body. Like it wasn't a fight to feel good."

She laughed softly. “And apparently, I cum twice now. That’s new.”

He grinned. “You’re an overachiever.”

She rolled her eyes, and he caught her chin between two fingers.

“I want to know what else you’d like to try.”

She blinked. “Really?”

“Yes. All of it. What you fantasize about. What makes you nervous. What you’re not sure you’re allowed to want.”

She smiled wide and real. “That list might be longer than you think.”

“I’m patient,” he said. “Dangerously so.”

Their laughter mixed with the candlelight.

He laid back beside her, pulling the sheet loosely over them both. She turned into him, resting her head on his chest. The soft thump of his heartbeat calmed something in her she hadn’t realized was still restless.

After a few moments of silence, he asked, “Do you want to go home tonight?”

She hesitated.

“I don’t have anything with me.”

“I don’t care.”

She looked up at him. “Do you want me to stay?”

His hand traced lazy circles on her back. “I want you to do whatever feels safe and good to you. But yes. I want you here.

If that’s what you want too.”

She nodded.

Then he kissed her once more and whispered, "Come on."

Still naked, they rose from the bed. He picked up a throw blanket from a chair and wrapped it around her shoulders.

He led her through the dim hallway and out onto a small balcony.

The night air was cool and sharp. The stars above were bright, scattered like diamonds.

They sat side by side on a cushioned bench, her legs draped over his lap, his arm around her shoulders.

Nothing needed to be said.

Not yet.

They just were.

Naked. Warm. Honest.

And for the first time in a long time...

She didn't want to be anywhere else.

Chapter 19

The Shift

Alessia's day started before the sun.

By 6:00 a.m., her phone was buzzing.

By 7:00, she'd already rescheduled two meetings, answered a minor crisis, and talked one junior employee off the ledge after a client meltdown.

By 8:15, she was in heels, seated at the head of the glasswalled conference room, fielding three voices at once while trying to breathe.

Emails. Texts. Phone calls.

Deadlines that had been moved without warning. People who couldn't seem to do what they promised. Mistakes that always, somehow, made their way back to her desk.

This was the part no one saw.

Yes, she ran the company. Yes, she was successful. But the pressure? The constant demand to fix things? It wore her down like waves on stone.

By mid-afternoon, her neck ached and her jaw was locked from clenching it.

She hadn't eaten. She hadn't breathed.

She hadn't felt anything that wasn't sharp or urgent in over twelve hours.

Until...

Her phone buzzed again.

Another fire?

No. Leander.

Her heart flipped, tripping over the stress in her chest.

Leander:

I want to steal you tonight.

No masks. No schedule. No one needing anything.

Just you. Me. A blanket under the stars.

Champagne. Strawberries. Something slow.

Say yes.

She closed her eyes.

Her body, still tight from stress, exhaled as if it had been waiting for those words all day.

Say yes.

She hit reply.

Yes.

Chapter 20

The Escape

The sun had just slipped below the horizon when Alessia arrived.

She spotted him in the clearing before he saw her.

A wide blanket had been spread across the grass beneath a canopy of trees, glowing softly in the fading twilight. Lanterns flickered at each corner, casting warm light over a simple but beautiful spread: champagne chilled in a silver bucket, ripe strawberries, thin slices of cheese and fruit, and a little jar of something dark and glossy.

Leander stood barefoot at the edge, sleeves rolled, hair slightly tousled, shirt open just enough to show that perfect line she always noticed above his waistband.

She stepped out of the trees.

He turned and his whole face changed.

"You're here," he said softly.

"I needed to be."

He reached for her hand and pulled her gently down onto the blanket.

There were no distractions. No phones. No pressure. Just him.

Them.

He poured champagne into delicate glasses, offered her a strawberry, then sat beside her.

"Tonight," he said, "I want you to taste everything. But with your eyes closed."

She raised an eyebrow. "That sounds dangerous."

He smirked. "That's the point."

She closed her eyes.

He fed her a piece of melon first. It was cool, wet, sweet.

"What does it taste like?" he asked.

"Clean. Bright. Like summer." She swallowed. "Like something I forgot I liked."

Next, a thin slice of cheese, rich and creamy. Then a strawberry dipped into the champagne... effervescent and sensual.

She bit into it, and a trickle of juice ran down her chin.

He caught it with his thumb, eyes dark. "You're beautiful like this."

Then he uncapped the jar.

Chocolate.

He dipped two fingers into the thick sauce and leaned over her.

Slowly, he brushed a warm line across the top of her breast.

She gasped.

"Close your eyes," he whispered. "Feel everything."

He painted more... down the curve of her belly, along her hip, the inside of her thigh.

Then he licked.

Slow.

Detailed.

Devoted.

She moaned, hands curling into the blanket, the air thick with scent and heat and the soft sounds of her breath.

When he returned to her mouth, he kissed her deeply, sharing the taste.

And then he handed her the whipped cream.

"Your turn," he said, voice low and thick. "Play with me."

She hesitated, then smiled. Shook the can lightly.

She sprayed a puff onto his lips and kissed it off, slow and lingering.

She dotted a swirl onto his chest, then licked it gently.

When she reached his nipple, she paused.

"Does it feel good for you?" she asked.

His breath caught.

"Yes."

She trailed more... down his chest, lower, following that line she always noticed.

And then... lower still.

She added a perfect stroke of cream.

And this time, she didn't just lick it off.

She took all of him.

Slow.

Intentional.

Watching his face, tasting everything.

He moaned, low and real, and tangled his hands in her hair.

And Alessia knew:

This wasn't just pleasure.

This was freedom.

Chapter 21

Beneath the Sky

The stars above them were silent witnesses.

Alessia lay on her back, her head resting on Leander's chest, the blanket tangled beneath their bare skin. The chocolate and fruit sat forgotten. The whipped cream can had rolled into the grass. Her lips were sticky. Her thighs trembled.

And she had never felt more at peace.

His hand stroked gently up and down her arm. No pressure.

Just presence.

"I don't usually..." she began, then stopped.

He waited.

She took a breath. "I don't usually let go like that."

He kissed her hair. "I know."

"No," she said. "I mean really let go. I'm always in charge. At work, with people, with expectations. Even in bed, I've always felt like I needed to... perform. Be perfect. Be... enough."

He didn't interrupt. Just listened.

"I've been through things," she said, voice softer now. "Things that made me afraid of my own body. Afraid to ask for more.

Afraid that wanting made me... cheap. Or weak."

He shifted slightly, rolling onto his side to face her. His fingers brushed her cheek, thumb tracing the soft curve of her lip.

“You’re not weak,” he said.

“You don’t even know—”

“I don’t have to know everything yet,” he said gently. “But I know what I see. I see a woman who holds the weight of a dozen people’s lives and doesn’t flinch. I see a woman who finally gave herself permission to want. And took it.”

She blinked.

“I see strength,” he continued. “I see fire. And I see softness.

And all of it, truly all of it, is allowed.”

She looked away. “Do you really believe that? That it’s okay to be both?”

“I don’t just believe it,” he said. “I crave it.”

A silence stretched between them... not empty, but full. Full of everything unspoken.

Then she reached for his hand.

“Thank you,” she whispered. “For tonight. For all of it.”

He kissed her fingertips, one by one.

“There’s more,” he said. “When you’re ready.”

“I think I’m getting there,” she said. “And I want you there with me.”

He smiled, slow and soft. “Good. Because I’m not going anywhere.”

They settled back into the blanket, the stars stretching wide above them.

But after a moment, Alessia sat up slightly, glancing toward the trees.

"Do you think..." she started, a teasing edge in her voice,

"someone might've seen us?"

Leander turned his head, one brow lifted. "Here? Possibly. It's public, after all."

Her eyes widened slightly, and then she laughed, surprised at herself.

"That should terrify me," she said. "A week ago, it would've."

"And now?"

She smiled. "Now... it kind of excites me."

He leaned up on one elbow, gaze intense. "Why?"

"Because I didn't feel ashamed. Not for how I looked. Not for how I sounded. Not even for how much I wanted you." She looked at him, her voice soft but sure. "You make me feel that way. Confident. Powerful. Sexy. Like I belong in this body."

Leander reached out and dragged his fingers slowly up her thigh. "You do. And if someone did see us?" He smirked.

"They were lucky."

She laughed again... deep, rich, full of something wild and alive.

"Maybe sometime soon," she said, voice low, "we don't wait until it's dark. Maybe we find somewhere a little less… hidden."

His eyes darkened instantly. "Tell me where. I'll bring the blanket."

Their kiss tasted like shared secrets.

And just like that, shame was no longer part of her vocabulary.

Chapter 22

The Man Behind the Control

(Leander's Point Of View))

Leander woke before the alarm. He always did.

He lay still for a moment, the early light slipping through the slats of the blinds. Alessia's scent was still on his skin. A whisper of her perfume lingered on the pillow beside him.

He ran a hand over his jaw and exhaled slowly.

She was under his skin.

And he wasn't in a rush to pull her out.

He got up, showered, and dressed. The routine grounded him... tailored slacks, crisp shirt, dark leather watch. No tie today. He wasn't expected anywhere specific. That was one of the luxuries of where he stood now.

In the kitchen of his penthouse, he made his espresso the way he liked it... strong, smooth, no sugar. As it brewed, he scrolled through morning reports from his companies. Logistics.

Investments. Updates on a luxury resort he was quietly developing overseas.

Everything was... fine. Clean. Functioning.

It always was.

He didn't have to be involved anymore, he'd built perfect systems and hired sharp people. But he liked to stay close to the edges. Not out of necessity.

Out of control.

He sipped his espresso and looked out across the city from thirty floors up. From here, the world looked orderly.

Predictable.

But last night with Alessia?

That had been anything but.

It wasn't just the way she tasted strawberries with her eyes closed, or the sound she made when he kissed her thighs. It was the way she let herself be seen. The way she let herself feel.

And the way she made him feel something deeper than he'd expected.

He wanted more of that.

More of her.

She wasn't a detour. She wasn't temporary.

His phone buzzed.

He expected a finance update or a vendor request.

Instead—Adrian.

His son.

Just one word popped up.

Emergency.

His chest tightened. He tapped the call.

"What happened?"

"Dad, I... I messed up."

Leander moved out onto the balcony, voice instantly calm.

"Where are you?"

"I'm fine. I just need you. I'm at your office. I didn't know where else to go."

"Okay. Sit tight. I'll be there in twenty."

He didn't ask for details yet. He didn't panic.

When he hung up, he ran a hand through his hair, exhaling hard through his nose.

His son was twenty-three. Brilliant. Complicated. Passionate.

Prone to recklessness.

Just like his mother.

Leander grabbed his keys and left, the lock clicking behind him.

The shift came easily, from lover to protector. From fantasy to reality. From soft hands to strong shoulders.

But even as the city blurred past the windows of his car,

Alessia remained.

The shape of her in the candlelight.

The sound of her moaning his name under the stars.

The softness of her gratitude. The boldness of her kiss.

She was still in his head.

Still on his skin.

And for the first time in a very long time...

he didn't mind one damn bit.

Chapter 23

The Dual World

Leander – Late Morning

Adrian looked pale, unsettled.

He sat on the edge of the couch in Leander's private office... shoulders hunched, fingers twisted in the hem of his shirt, like he was fifteen again instead of twenty-three.

Leander stood by the window, arms folded. "Talk to me."

Adrian inhaled. "It's the production team in L.A. They mismanaged the inventory rollout. I didn't catch it in time. The shipping costs tripled overnight, and now one of the retail partners wants to walk."

Leander stayed quiet, letting his son get the panic out.

Adrian went on. "I tried to fix it. I called everyone. But I... I needed help. I didn't know who else to go to."

Leander finally spoke, calm as ever. "You came to the right place."

Adrian looked up, his eyes rimmed red. Not from tears, but from pressure. "You're not mad?"

Leander crossed the room and sat beside him. "No. You're learning. And you're here, that matters more than fixing everything alone."

Adrian nodded, swallowing hard.

Together, they outlined the next steps. A restructuring of the agreement. A quiet conversation with the retail contact.

Leander made two phone calls, said a few key words, and the dominoes began to realign.

Within an hour, the crisis was in motion to be resolved.

Adrian leaned back in the chair, the tension slowly leaving his frame. “I feel like I can breathe again.”

“You should. You’ll mess up again,” Leander said with a faint smirk. “But you’ll recover faster next time.”

Adrian laughed once... tired, but genuine.

As Leander stood and grabbed his keys again, Adrian looked up.

“Thanks, Dad. I mean it.”

Leander paused in the doorway. “Always.”

Alessia – That Same Afternoon

Alessia sat at her desk, fingers hovering above her phone screen.

No text.

No message.

Not a word from Leander since the night in the park. No morning-after check-in. No teasing line. No “still thinking of you.”

She wasn’t panicking.

Not exactly.

But she noticed.

And in the quiet space between meetings, between deadlines and distractions, she opened her messages and started to type:

Hey... just thinking about last night. Hope you're good.

Her thumb hovered over "send."

Then she hit backspace.

Paused.

Deleted the whole thing.

She wasn't going to be that woman. The one who clings. Who reads silence as rejection.

Still...

She stood, walked to the window, and looked out at the lateday sun sliding down the buildings.

She had work. She had a life.

She just didn't expect it to feel... this quiet without him.

⊡

Leander – Dusk

As soon as Leander slid back into his car, he pulled out his phone.

No hesitation.

Just instinct.

He opened their thread, tapped the keyboard, and typed slowly:

Leander:

I didn't disappear. Just needed to take care of someone who needed me.

Still thinking about you. Especially the way you tasted last night.

He hit send.

And smiled, just slightly.

Because for the first time in years, someone else was on his mind, even when the world was falling apart.

And that someone... was worth every second.

Chapter 24

The Message

Alessia's phone buzzed on her desk.

She glanced at the screen, and froze.

Leander.

She opened the message.

I didn't disappear. Just needed to take care of someone who needed me.

Still thinking about you. Especially the way you tasted last night.

A soft breath left her lungs. Then a smile curved her lips, unexpected and warm.

She laughed, quiet and to herself.

God, you were really about to spiral, she thought. Over a few hours of silence.

But that's what this was starting to become, something she noticed when it was missing.

She sat back, still smiling, and typed her reply:

I'm glad it wasn't me you had to rescue this time.

Is everything okay now?

She stared at the screen for a second, debating if it sounded too much like she cared.

You do care, she reminded herself.

She hit send.

Moments later, three dots appeared.

Leander:

Everything's handled. It was my son. He's alright now. But I've been thinking about you all day.

Her chest warmed again. The mention of his son softened something in her, made him feel even more real... not just fantasy, but flesh and family.

Another message followed before she could reply:

What are you doing tomorrow night?

Because I don't want to go another day without seeing you.

She bit her lip, heart fluttering.

Typed back:

Tomorrow night sounds perfect.

What do you have in mind?

And then his next message came through—

That depends on what you're in the mood for...

Because I plan on giving it to you.

—she leaned back in her chair, the rest of her day suddenly a little easier to face.

Chapter 25

Something Special

Alessia took the long way home.

Not because she had to but because her mind was buzzing.

Leander was coming over. No reservations. No distractions.

Just the two of them. One night. Something slow.

She stopped at a boutique on impulse, drawn to a soft gold slip dress in the window. With thin straps, a cowl neckline, and a hem that flirted with the top of her thighs. It clung in all the right places, barely skimming the rest.

Flirty. Sexy. Just dressed-up enough to get away with.

She paired it with a subtle gloss, a soft heel, and a quiet confidence she hadn't worn in years.

⊡

He arrived with groceries in one arm and a bottle of wine in the other.

"No apron?" he teased, glancing at her dress.

She smirked. "No need. You're the one doing the messy work."

They started the cooking together... cutting, stirring, sipping.

The kitchen filled with the scent of garlic and her laughter.

He leaned in behind her at the stove once, one hand on her waist, the other stirring the sauce. She could feel his breath on her neck, his body warm against hers.

“You’re doing this on purpose,” she said.

“What, cooking?”

“No. Driving me crazy.”

He smiled without looking up. “That’s just a bonus.”

Dinner was simple. Pasta. Salad. Wine. But it felt like something else... like a promise in motion.

They sat close, knees brushing. She told him a story about her most embarrassing date. He told her about the time he burned rice in front of a Michelin-star chef. They laughed. Touched.

Lingered.

But then she reached for her glass, and he leaned to take her plate.

In a blink, red wine tipped forward.

It spilled over the front of her dress, soaking into the gold silk and leaving a deep stain across her chest.

She gasped.

He froze.

Then smiled.

“Looks like I’m cleaning up after all.”

She laughed, half-startled, half-thrilled. “You better. I love this dress.”

“It’s not the dress I’m focused on,” he murmured, his fingers already tracing the wet edge at her collarbone.

She looked up at him, breath catching.

"Shower?" he asked, his voice low, velvet over heat.

She nodded once.

He took her hand.

Chapter 26

Heat Rising

Leander turned on the water, adjusting it warm, just shy of hot.

Alessia stood behind him, her chest rising and falling with anticipation.

The bathroom filled with steam almost instantly.

He turned, facing her.

Neither of them said a word.

She slipped the dress over her head slowly, letting it fall to the tile with a soft whisper. No bra. Just her skin glowing, damp from the heat in the air.

His eyes darkened.

She stepped into the shower first, letting the water cascade over her body, soaking her hair, trickling down between her breasts, her stomach, her thighs. She tilted her face to the stream and let out a small, content sound.

Then he stepped in behind her.

The heat of his body added to the warmth of the water. His hands slowly ran down her back, open-palmed, reverent.

Their bodies touched, slick and bare. Such a feeling of peace and pleasure at the same time.

She turned to face him, nipples already taut under the gentle spray. Water glistened over his chest, trailing down the sharp lines of his abs.

Then lower.

Her eyes followed. So did her hands.

His cock was already thick and rising between them.

She looked up at him as she dropped to her knees, water cascading over her back. She never broke eye contact.

Her hands wrapped around him, one holding firm at the base, the other stroking up his thigh. She licked just the tip first, playful and teasing, then circled it with her tongue.

He groaned, deep and low, his head tipping back against the tile.

She took him deeper, her mouth warm and soft, moving slowly, her hand gliding in rhythm with her lips. The other hand kept exploring... his thigh, his hip, the curve of his ass.

Water splashed onto her face, mixing with his taste.

His hand slid into her wet hair, gently not guiding or forcing, his thumb tracing the line of her jaw.

"Alessia..." he breathed.

But he didn't want to come like this.

Not yet.

He pulled back gently, and she let him.

Then, without a word, he lifted her effortlessly.

Her back pressed to the shower wall, her legs wrapped around his waist. His tip found her entrance, already wet, already open, and with one smooth thrust—

He filled her.

Completely.

She cried out, nails digging into his shoulders. He held her steady, driving in slow at first, then deeper, more insistent.

Their mouths met... wet, frantic, hungry.

The steam cloaked them, blurred everything except the way they moved together. His cock stroked inside her with aching precision. Her hips rocked, chasing the rhythm, needing more.

But he wasn't done.

He turned off the water, the sound of the spray silencing in an instant, and stepped out. Still inside her, carrying her like something sacred.

They moved to the oversized chair by the window. He laid her down gently, her hair damp and wild across the cushion.

He knelt between her legs.

"Let me taste you," he said.

She nodded, breathless.

He lowered his mouth, licking the water away first, then replacing it with something hotter. His tongue moved slow, skillful, coaxing her open again.

She moaned, hands in his hair.

When he rose over her again, his cock slick between them, he rubbed the length of it along her folds... up and down, teasing, tempting.

She arched, desperate.

"Now," she whispered.

And he gave her everything.

Chapter 27

More Than Heat

The lights were low.

Only the faintest golden wash from the street below filtered through the windows, tracing soft lines across their bare skin.

Alessia lay half-draped over Leander's chest, her cheek against the smooth, warm plane of him. Her legs tangled with his. One hand rested just below his collarbone, fingers trailing lazy circles without thought.

His arm curled around her shoulders. The other lay across his stomach, his thumb absently stroking her hip.

They hadn't said anything for several minutes.

But it wasn't silence.

It was peace.

She could still feel him inside her, even though he wasn't. The ache, the fullness, the imprint.

She felt him everywhere.

"Is this..." she began, then stopped, her voice quiet.

He didn't press. Just waited.

She turned her head, looking up at him. "Is this becoming something more than... you know. Heat?"

His brow ticked, but his lips curved faintly. "You mean, are we still pretending this is casual?"

She smirked. "We were never good at pretending."

He tilted his head toward her. “No. You were too honest with your eyes.”

She smiled, but it softened into something more vulnerable. “I don’t want to mess this up.”

“You won’t.”

She looked at him fully now. “I’ve never let anyone in like this.

Not this close. Not physically and emotionally. At the same time.”

“I know,” he said. “That’s why I’m still here.”

They laid there a moment longer, the words heavy but comforting between them.

Then she said, almost teasing, “Do your friends know about me?”

His eyes sparkled. “Not yet. Why, are you hoping for a dinner invite?”

She laughed. “Maybe.”

“Well,” he said, running a hand slowly along her thigh, “I have a couple of friends who’d be intrigued that I’m spending more time naked than in meetings.”

She rolled her eyes, then paused. “What about you? Want to meet mine?”

“Are they as direct as you?”

She gave him a mock serious look. “Absolutely.”

“I’m in,” he said, smiling wide. “But only if I get to tell them the real story about how we met.”

She laughed. “If you do that, I’ll have to explain what it means to be tied to a chair and blindfolded with a silk mask.”

He leaned down and kissed her shoulder. “You say that like it’s a bad thing.”

“No,” she murmured, tucking herself closer into him. “It’s just… a beginning.”

He nodded, and they let the quiet return, this time full of something new.

Not tension.

Not lust.

But promise.

Chapter 28
First Glimpse

The café was tucked into a quiet side street. One of those places that smelled like cinnamon and roasted espresso, with handwritten menus and too many plants hanging from the ceiling.

Alessia arrived first.

She wore something soft and fitted, casual but intentional. Her heart beat just a little faster than normal, but not from fear.

More like anticipation.

She was about to meet his people.

Not a blindfold. Not a whispered command.

Just conversation. Just real life.

She tucked a strand of hair behind her ear and tried not to replay every word from the night before. Or the night before that.

When Leander walked in, he didn't just look confident, he looked proud.

He kissed her cheek softly, placed a hand on the small of her back, and guided her toward the table.

"They're already here," he said. "And they're going to love you."

She gave him a side glance. "You say that like it's guaranteed."

"It is."

Seated at the back were two people... a man and a woman, both dressed effortlessly, like they belonged in some artful magazine spread.

“Alessia,” Leander said, hand still on her back, “this is Marc and Delia.”

Marc stood, shook her hand with a warm smile. “So you’re the one who’s been distracting him.”

Delia laughed. “It’s about time someone did.”

Alessia flushed, but not with embarrassment. It was something else. A thrill. An ease she didn’t expect.

They sat. Coffee was poured. Small talk began.

And she realized something: they weren’t judging her. They weren’t picking her apart.

They were watching Leander.

And he was watching her.

Every now and then, his hand would graze hers under the table.

Or his knee would press softly against hers.

A silent reassurance.

A shared secret.

At one point, Marc leaned forward. “So, what do you do when you’re not keeping this man on his toes?”

Alessia smiled. “Manage chaos. And occasionally let myself be led into it.”

Delia grinned. “Sounds like a match made in madness.”

It was light. Playful.

But somewhere beneath it, there was a shift.

She wasn't just Alessia anymore.

She was his Alessia.

And for the first time, she didn't feel like she was stepping into someone else's world.

She felt like she was building one with him.

Chapter 29

Fair Trade

The evening at the café stretched longer than expected.

Conversation came easy. The laughter even easier.

Alessia found herself liking Marc and Delia more than she wanted to admit. Not because they were charming, though they were, but because of how naturally they fit with Leander.

How well they knew him. How much they seemed to care about him.

She could tell they noticed the way he looked at her.

And that they approved.

As they stood to say goodbye, Delia leaned in and whispered,

"You're good for him. Don't let him forget it."

Alessia smiled. "I don't plan to."

When they stepped back into the evening air, Leander's hand slipped easily into hers.

"That wasn't too painful, was it?" he asked, guiding her down the sidewalk.

"Not at all," she said. "In fact, I think I passed."

He grinned. "Flying colors."

She nudged him. "You know what this means, right?"

His brow lifted. "What?"

"Your turn."

She smirked. "It's only fair."

⊡

They planned it two days later.

A cozy wine bar with soft lighting and a corner table just private enough.

Alessia arrived first, wearing a fitted black dress and a shade of red lipstick that made Leander's mouth twitch the second he saw her.

At the table sat two women... one with striking resemblance to

Alessia, the other with eyes that missed nothing and a wine glass already half-full.

Leander leaned down and kissed Alessia's cheek. "So... this is the firing squad?"

Alessia smiled. "Be charming. Or at least try."

She turned. "Leander, this is my sister, Bianca. And my best friend, Tessa."

Bianca stood and hugged him without hesitation. Tessa extended her hand, eyes assessing but curious.

They sat.

And within minutes, the questions began.

"So," Tessa started, "you're clearly successful, smooth, and apparently know how to make pasta from scratch. Why are you still single?"

Leander didn't flinch. "I was busy building. And waiting."

Bianca raised an eyebrow. "Waiting?"

He glanced at Alessia. "For her."

That earned him a nod of approval. And a refill of everyone's glasses.

The rest of the evening flowed easily. More stories, more teasing, more laughter.

And then, near the end, the music picked up.

A slow, sultry rhythm.

Bianca smirked and nudged Alessia. "He said he can cook... but can he dance?"

Leander was already standing, offering his hand with a quiet confidence. "Want to find out?"

They swayed in time, bodies close.

Alessia leaned into him, her hand warm against his chest.

"You're good," she murmured.

"Better than expected?"

"Much."

They moved slowly, letting the music carry them, letting their world expand... one new person, one soft rhythm at a time.

It didn't feel like pressure and routine.

It didn't feel like a test.

It felt natural and easy.

It felt like the beginning of something real.

Chapter 30

The Reveal

They didn't go out after the dancing.

No late-night drink. No nightcap at the bar.

Instead, Alessia let Leander take her hand and guide her home, his thumb brushing slow circles against her skin as they walked. The silence between them wasn't heavy. It pulsed with something unspoken. Something waiting.

By the time they reached her apartment, her breath was already shallow.

She unlocked the door, stepped inside, and turned to him. But he was already looking at her with that unreadable expression, the one he wore when he was about to ask something deeper.

She knew it.

Felt it.

He closed the door behind them, then leaned his back to it.

"I want to ask you something," he said.

She nodded. "Okay."

"But first, I want to tell you something. And I don't know if it's going to come out right."

She stepped closer, quiet. "Try."

He looked at her for a long moment. Then:

“I thought I was done with real connection. Not because I didn’t want it, but because I didn’t trust it. People see what I have. They fall in love with the surface.”

He paused.

“You didn’t.”

She swallowed, her heart catching.

“You saw the man. Not the name. Not the money. Not the charm. And I didn’t realize how starved I was for that until I met you.”

Alessia’s chest tightened.

“I thought I needed control,” she said softly. “In every part of my life. But you... made me feel safe letting go. I didn’t think that was possible anymore.”

He stepped forward now, slow, steady, until they were face to face.

“Then let go now.”

She did.

Her mouth found his.

The kiss wasn’t rushed. It didn’t burn.

It ached.

She pulled him in, and he walked her back toward the bedroom, unbuttoning his shirt with each step. She stripped the heels from her feet, her dress sliding over her hips and pooling at her ankles.

By the time they reached the bed, they were skin to skin.

He laid her down with care, crawling over her like a promise.

This wasn't hunger.

This was reverence.

When he entered her, it was slow. Purposeful. Each movement syncing with her breath, her sighs, her fingers clinging to his back. Their bodies moved in rhythm, eyes locked, lips brushing.

She came quietly. He followed with a groan against her throat.

And for a long time after, they didn't move.

Only breathed.

Only felt.

⊡

Later, as they lay tangled beneath the sheets, Alessia's hand on his chest and his fingers tracing her arm, Leander spoke again.

"I want you to come with me."

She looked up, blinking.

"To the coast. Where the resort is. It's still being restored but it's fully functional. I go there sometimes to meet with the team. It's quiet. Beautiful. Far from everything."

She blinked again, unsure if he meant vacation or something more.

"You don't have to decide now," he added. "But I want you there. With me."

Alessia smiled, soft and slow. "Then maybe... I want that too."

Chapter 31

Arrival

The moment Alessia stepped off the private transfer van, her breath caught.

The air was warm but not heavy. Fragrant with something floral and salty, like hibiscus and sea spray. The breeze kissed her skin as if the island already knew her name.

They had landed less than an hour ago, somewhere along the sun-drenched coast of southern Europe, he hadn't mentioned exactly where. Just that it was quiet, exclusive, and the kind of place where you can forget the world.

He hadn't lied.

The resort stretched across the bluff like something pulled from a dream. Stone paths lined with beautiful flowers, open-air terraces, and sleek modern villas tucked into the landscape like secrets.

As they approached the main building, staff appeared instantly with warm smiles, subtle bows, champagne flutes offered without a word.

"Mr. Moore," one of them said, inclining her head respectfully.

Alessia looked up at him, slightly stunned. "Mr. Moore?"

He leaned in close, his voice a warm tease. "They don't call me

Leander here. They call me the man who helped fund paradise."

She raised a brow. "Should I start curtsying?"

"Only if you want the royal treatment."

She didn't have to ask for her luggage. It vanished. Nor did she need to check in,everything was seamless. Silent. Handled.

And then he led her to the villa.

The door opened, and her heart nearly stopped.

The suite was enormous. Airy. Every surface smooth and cool, kissed by natural light. The bed was a California king, draped in soft white linen, with a sheer canopy that stirred gently in the breeze from the open balcony doors.

Double sinks lined the bathroom vanity, lit by gold-framed mirrors and flanked by fresh orchids. Beyond the doors, the private balcony offered a view of pale sand and endless ocean.

There was a table with two cushioned chairs. A pair of loungers angled toward the water. And down below, just beyond the palm-dotted edge of the resort, Alessia caught sight of something else.

A nude beach.

She blinked.

Leander, already loosening the buttons of his shirt, followed her gaze.

"Tempting, isn't it?"

She turned slowly toward him. "Is that... optional?"

He shrugged, eyes glinting. "Only if you want it to be."

"And have you—?"

"I've tried it," he said. "It's freeing. And fun. But only if you're ready. I'd never push."

She looked back out toward the sand, heart fluttering.

"Decide later," he said, stepping behind her and brushing a kiss along her neck. "You've got all the time in the world here."

She leaned into him, his warmth against her back, the view stretching endlessly before them.

It was already the most beautiful place she'd ever been.

And it wasn't just the beach. Or the view. Or the perfect villa.

It was the way he touched her like they had all the time in the world.

Chapter 32

Letting Go

The spa was unlike anything Alessia had ever seen.

They entered through a corridor of flickering lanterns and the soft sound of trickling water. The scent of jasmine and something warm, amber maybe, wrapped around her like a second skin.

She glanced at Leander, who looked entirely at ease, already speaking quietly to the attendant in a language she couldn't place.

Before she could ask, the woman smiled at Alessia. "You'll be in the couples' retreat today. Full service. Please follow me."

They were led into a private sanctuary. The ceiling arched high overhead, with skylights that let sunlight pour across polished stone and sheer white drapery that danced gently in the breeze.

Two massage tables. A warm plunge pool. A bowl of rose petals floating nearby.

"Undress to your comfort," the attendant said with a bow.

"We'll begin shortly."

Alessia paused.

Leander stepped behind her, his fingers brushing her hip.

"We don't have to," he whispered. "But I think you deserve this."

She met his eyes.

"I want to."

They undressed slowly. Her skin tingling from the change in temperature, from his gaze, from her own daring.

The massage began with warm oil, firm hands, slow rhythm.

The therapists worked in near silence, only the gentle murmur of waves and wind outside filling the space.

She felt her body melt into the table, breath deepening, tension sliding off her shoulders with every stroke.

When it was done, she floated in the heated plunge pool beside

Leander, her legs draped over his lap, his fingers trailing softly over her thighs.

"How do you feel?" he asked.

She closed her eyes. "Loose. Melted. Like honey."

"Good," he murmured, leaning in to kiss the side of her neck.

"That was the point."

⊡

They dressed again in lightweight linen provided by the spa. Effortless, comfortable, and sensual without trying.

By the time they reached the open-air bar on the far side of the resort, the sun was low and golden, casting long amber shadows across the floor.

They sat in a quiet corner with plush chairs and a view of the beach. A small candle flickered between them.

She ordered something sweet and floral. He ordered whiskey.

They clinked glasses.

“To whatever comes next,” she said.

He watched her over the rim of his glass. “Are you ready for what comes next?”

“I think...” she smiled slowly, “I’m ready to find out.”

He leaned forward, his voice velvet-smooth. “And if what comes next is a little... uninhibited?”

She took another sip of her drink. Let it burn just a little.

“Then maybe I’ll stop holding back.”

Chapter 33

Moonlit Temptation

The ocean whispered beneath a silver moon. The night air was cool, refreshing against their skin, as Alessia and Leander strolled barefoot along the edge of the resort's private beach.

They didn't speak at first.

Their hands brushed now and then, not quite linked. The surf rolled in quietly, kissing the sand, then sliding away like a sigh.

It was quiet and open and impossibly free.

Leander broke the silence with a sideways glance and a glint of mischief in his eye. "So... have you decided?"

Alessia didn't need to ask what he meant.

She had seen the nude beach that very first day from their balcony. The soft, unspoiled curve of it tucked beyond the palms, its air of secrecy and boldness. He hadn't explained much. He hadn't needed to. Just a teasing smile and a wellplaced suggestion.

Since then, it had lingered in her mind like the edge of a dream.

She smiled. "Maybe."

He let the word hang there, loose and light.

"No pressure," he said. "But if you're going to be bold, I wouldn't mind being there to witness it."

She gave him a look... half playful, half knowing. "Of course you wouldn't."

He chuckled, brushing his knuckles along the small of her back as they walked.

“There’s something about shedding every layer that doesn’t belong to you anymore,” he said. “Something... freeing.”

She looked out at the moonlit horizon, the stars reflected in the water, the endless stretch of openness ahead. “I’ve spent most of my life wearing things that made everyone else comfortable.”

He nodded. “Not here.”

“No,” she said softly. “Not here.”

They walked a little farther. The air was filled with salt and warmth and something more charged... anticipation.

Then she stopped and turned to face him.

“Not tonight,” she said. “But maybe tomorrow. When the light is new. When it feels like a beginning.”

He stepped in closer, the space between them melting.

“Then tomorrow,” he whispered, brushing her lips with a soft kiss. “I’ll be right beside you.”

She nodded, her heart steady now. Not racing. Not unsure.

Just... ready.

They turned back slowly, hands now fully linked as they strolled up the sand. The moon rose higher behind them, casting two long shadows that moved in step, like they’d been walking this way all along.

Chapter 34

The Naked Truth

The sun was just rising when they reached the beach.

Golden light spilled across the horizon, turning the waves to fire and the sand to silk. The air was warm with promise, still quiet enough to feel sacred.

They walked together without speaking.

Alessia's heart beat calmly, no panic or hesitation, just steady anticipation as they made their way to a quiet stretch of the resort's private nude beach. The same curve of sand she'd seen from the balcony now shimmered before her like a secret waiting to be claimed.

Two loungers waited, half in the sun, half in shadow.

She paused.

Then, without ceremony or fanfare, she untied the soft linen wrap she'd worn and let it fall.

No bikini.

No barriers.

Just her.

The breeze kissed her skin as if it had been waiting. The sunlight draped her body like a blessing.

She lay down on the lounger... bare, open, alive. Every inch of her touched the air, the light, the moment. There was no rush to cover. No instinct to shrink. Only the sensation of sun on her breasts, her stomach, her thighs. It felt... right.

Free.

She turned her head and saw Leander.

Already nude, already beside her, his body relaxed, his expression soft. He looked at her with reverence, not hunger.

He didn't reach for her.

He didn't have to.

She reached for him instead, tracing a slow, tender path along the inside of his forearm, just to feel him.

To remind herself this was real.

And then, just for a moment, she let her fingers drift lower.

A quiet touch across his hip.

He inhaled, deep and controlled. His hand found the top of her thigh and stroked upward slowly, lightly, until his fingertips grazed the delicate, sensitive place between her legs.

Her breath caught.

Not from surprise but from how natural it felt. How wanted.

How true.

She turned toward him, letting her hand trail down his stomach.

Her fingers wrapped briefly around the base of him... warm, alive, already growing under her touch.

Just one stroke.

A pause.

The world didn't stop.

No one looked their way.

And in that heat, the sunlight on her bare skin, his body beside hers, their hands teasing at the edge of something more... she felt a hunger bloom from deep inside her.

She wanted him.

There.

Right there, in full daylight. With the breeze on her skin and no fabric between them. With nothing hidden, nothing restrained.

She wanted him completely.

And not because she needed to feel desired...

But because she finally knew what it meant to desire without apology.

In that moment... raw, glowing, and wholly herself—

She knew she loved him.

Chapter 35

The Last Full Day

The sun was higher now.

Alessia stood by the balcony window, wrapped in a thin cotton robe, her skin still warm from the beach, her mind wrapped in something quieter.

Clarity.

There was something about being seen so fully, naked not just in body but in essence, and still feeling safe, even... wanted.

Not for performance, or perfection.

Just as she was.

She thought she would feel shy afterward. Embarrassed. But instead, she felt strong. Like the Alessia she had been shaping inside herself had finally stepped out into the light.

Behind her, Leander moved easily through the suite, barefoot, relaxed. The way he looked at her hadn't changed, but now she believed it.

That was the difference.

They spent the morning wandering the hillside trails above the resort, sipping espresso from a quiet terrace that overlooked the endless sea. Locals nodded at Leander with familiarity, staff greeted her like she'd always belonged.

But it wasn't the resort that made it feel like a fairytale.

It was how she moved now... without apology.

At one point, he brushed his hand against the small of her back, and she leaned into it naturally. She didn't look around. She didn't wonder what anyone thought. She just felt.

⊡

That afternoon, they returned to the villa. Alessia ran a warm bath, dropped in something floral, and sank into the water with a satisfied sigh. Leander brought her a glass of wine and left her to soak in silence.

Later, they lay side by side again, not on the beach this time, but on the shaded balcony. She wore nothing. Neither did he.

Their bodies touched in quiet ways. His hand resting on her stomach, her foot against his calf, her head against his shoulder.

"I've never felt like this," she said softly, not needing to define it.

He didn't ask her to.

That night, they shared a final dinner in a quiet corner of the resort's restaurant. Candles flickered low. A soft breeze swept through.

No plans.

No tension.

Just gratitude.

At the end of the meal, as they walked hand in hand through the dimly lit path back toward their villa, Alessia stopped.

"I don't want to forget this," she said.

"You won't."

"I don't want to lose... me, either."

Leander turned toward her, brushing a hand along her jaw.

"Then don't. Bring her home with you."

She smiled. "She's never been this sure of herself."

"She has," he said. "She just hadn't met someone who deserved her yet."

Chapter 36

Return

The wheels touched down just past sunset.

City lights glittered beneath the... familiar, fast-paced, humming with responsibility. Alessia stared out the plane window, watching the skyline approach, feeling the weight of reentry settle across her shoulders.

But this time, it didn't feel heavy.

She wasn't stepping back into a life she'd outgrown.

She was stepping forward into it, as someone new.

Leander glanced over and reached for her hand. No words. Just a squeeze. Reassuring. Grounding.

They didn't speak much on the ride to her apartment. The silence wasn't awkward. It was thoughtful. Reflective.

The kind of quiet that happens between people who don't need to fill space to be close.

When they pulled up in front of her building, Leander stepped out first, then circled around to open her door. She smiled as she slid out of the seat, eyes searching his.

"Are you coming up?"

He leaned in, his mouth brushing hers. "If you'll have me."

⊡

Her apartment hadn't changed, but she had.

Even the way she walked through it was different. She moved with purpose now. With ownership.

Leander placed her bag by the door and looked around like he was stepping into a new space, too. As if everything felt just a little brighter now.

She pulled off her coat and stood by the window.

He came up behind her, wrapped his arms around her waist, and kissed her neck. “Home,” he murmured.

And it was.

But it wasn’t the end.

Chapter 37

Bound to Trust

Two weeks later, Alessia stood in front of her mirror in a silk robe the color of midnight.

She had invited him over.

But tonight wasn't about dinner. Or unwinding. Or even talking.

It was about exploration.

Beside her on the bed: a blindfold, a single velvet ribbon, and one piece of dark chocolate.

She thought back to the beach. The sun on her bare skin. The way his hands had touched her in full daylight, with no hesitation. The way she had wanted him there, with no shame.

And she knew they weren't finished there.

She wanted to go back.

Not just to that resort, but to that freedom.

To discover what it meant to surrender completely, with someone who knew how to hold her.

Her phone buzzed.

Leander:

I'm downstairs.

She smiled.

Everything inside her sparked.

And as she picked up the ribbon and turned toward the door, she thought *I'm ready.*

She heard the knock before she'd finished breathing.

The silk robe still clung to her shoulders. The blindfold lay on the bed where she'd placed it deliberately and unashamed. The velvet ribbon coiled beside it like a question she'd already answered. On the nightstand, a single piece of dark chocolate rested on a small white plate.

She crossed to the door and opened it.

Leander stood in the hallway, still in his jacket, his eyes dropping once to the robe, the candlelight behind her, then back to her face. He didn't speak. He just looked at her the way he always did. Like she'd done something remarkable simply by existing.

"You actually set it up," he said quietly.

"I said I would."

He stepped inside.

She closed the door.

The apartment was warm and dim, the candles she'd lit burning low, their flames swaying gently with the music she'd chosen. He noticed all of it. She watched him notice.

"Tell me what you want," he said.

She picked up the blindfold and held it out to him.

"I want to feel everything," she said. "Without seeing it coming."

He took it from her fingers slowly.

"You trust me."

It wasn't a question. But she answered anyway.

"Yes."

He moved behind her and she felt his hands gather her hair, lifting it gently off her neck before the silk settled over her eyes. The world went dark, not frightening, but full. Every sound sharpened. The soft pull of the ribbon as he tied it. The warmth of his breath near her ear. The whisper of his jacket as he set it aside.

She felt him step in front of her.

His hands found her shoulders first, unhurried and grounding. Then the belt of her robe loosened with one slow pull. The fabric slid from her and she stood bare in the candlelight she could no longer see, and felt, for a long suspended moment, like something sacred.

"You're beautiful," he said. Low. Certain.

She didn't deflect it this time.

She just received it.

He guided her back to the edge of the bed. She heard him reach for the nightstand.

The chocolate touched her lips. Dark. Bitter-sweet. Placed there with his fingers, his thumb lingering at the corner of her mouth as she bit softly into it. The taste bloomed across her tongue, rich and slow.

She exhaled.

"Wrists," he said softly.

She offered them.

The velvet ribbon was loose, more as a suggestion than restraint. She could have slipped free easily, and they both knew it. That wasn't the point. The point was the choosing. The staying.

He cupped her breasts, thumbs brushing over her nipples with practiced care. She felt every pass, slowly and deliberately, building the tension like he knew exactly where it lived in her body.

And he did.

Her pulse thundered in her neck. Her thighs clenched. She felt the heat rising.

"Leander," she whispered, tilting her head, needing more.

He turned her gently, kneeling in front of her.

She couldn't see him. But she felt his presence... close, warm, his breath against her skin.

Her own breath hitched.

"Taste me," she said, her voice shaking but sure.

He looked up at her, she felt it even through the dark, and then he did.

His mouth was slow at first. Soft. He kissed her like she was the only thing he'd ever crave again. His tongue moved with intention, coaxing every gasp and tremor from her body.

Her bound wrists strained as her head fell back and her legs shook.

He held her there with firm hands on her hips, grounding her, guiding her, worshiping her.

She was already unraveling when he rose to his feet.

Still silent, he turned her gently. Not rough. Not hurried.

Just firm.

Just sure.

Her knees met the edge of the couch.

He bent her forward, hands braced on the cushions, skin exposed, breath catching in her throat. His hand reached around, teasing her breasts again. Rolling her nipple between his fingers, slow and sure.

And then a sharp slap to her ass.

She flinched, instinctively.

But then he rubbed the same spot slowly. Lovingly. Caressed it with his palm. Let her breathe through it.

"Again?" he asked, voice steady and kind.

She hesitated.

"Do you like it?" she whispered.

"No, Alessia," he said, moving in close, his chest brushing her back. "Do you like it? Do you want more?"

She closed her eyes. Her whole body alive.

"Yes."

His hand moved again.

And this time, she didn't flinch.

She moaned.

He leaned forward, his voice low at her neck. "Good girl."

Her "yes" still lingered in the air, barely more than a whisper, but full of weight. Full of want.

He didn't hesitate.

His hand came down again, a crisp smack across the same spot. She gasped, but this time her body pushed back into his palm, as if seeking more.

He soothed the sting immediately, rubbing soft circles into the warmth he'd left behind.

"You liked that," he murmured.

She nodded, breath shaky. "I think... I did."

He leaned in, pressing a kiss between her shoulder blades. "We'll go slow."

Then he guided himself into her.

One long, controlled thrust.

She moaned, the sound torn from her throat, raw and real. The fullness. The stretch. The vulnerable position. Her hands still bound, chest pressed to the back of the couch, completely open to him.

He filled her completely.

Paused.

Let her feel all of him.

Then moved.

His pace was deliberate... deep, slow, and grounding. With every thrust her body rocked forward, and his hands caught her hips, guiding her back again. She melted into it, her voice trembling with every breath.

"You're incredible," he said, groaning against her neck.

Her bound hands gave her no leverage. She surrendered to the rhythm. To him. To herself.

He reached around and cupped her breast again, pinching gently, rolling her nipple between his fingers. His other hand slipped lower, stroking the slick heat between her thighs. The pressure. The motion. All of it too much and still not enough.

"Leander..."

She was breathless. Breaking.

He kissed her shoulder, his voice low and rough. "Say it again."

"Yes."

And again, he spanked her, slightly harder.

She cried out, but the sound was a moan wrapped in a gasp.

The pleasure twisted. Built. Changed her from the inside out.

He didn't stop. His rhythm unrelenting, his hand a blur between her legs. She clenched around him, pulsing, spiraling into release so hard she couldn't hold back the sound that tore free from her.

Her body shook, legs trembling beneath her, the orgasm crashing through her in waves.

And even as she collapsed forward, his hands were gentle again. Untying her wrists, kissing the reddened skin, whispering her name.

He turned her slowly, carefully, gathering her into his lap as he sat back on the couch. She climbed over him, straddling his thighs, arms wrapping around his neck.

Then she sank onto him again.

Skin to skin.

Eye to eye.

Soft now. Slow.

Real.

She rode him with languid, rolling movements. Savoring every thrust, every inch of him, her lips brushing his between gasps. He cupped her jaw. Brushed her hair behind her ear.

When he came, it was deep and quiet. His forehead pressed to hers, their bodies shaking in time.

And still she didn't let go of him.

She curled into his chest, her bound wrists now free, her arms wrapped around him, their bodies still connected in the warm and quiet dark.

Then, without warning —

A single tear slipped down her cheek.

Not from sadness.

Not even from joy.

But from something deeper, a quiet recognition. A letting go. A becoming.

He felt it.

He didn't ask why.

He only tightened his arms around her, pressing a kiss to the crown of her head.

She didn't wipe the tear away.

"Thank you," she whispered against his chest.

He knew.

It wasn't for the sex. It wasn't for the pleasure or even the freedom. It was for something far more sacred. For seeing her. For not flinching when she unraveled. For holding every part of her — every contradiction, every fear, every edge — with reverence instead of restraint.

He pressed his lips to her temple, his voice a low hum against her skin.

"You're safe with me."

And she was.

The candles burned lower.

And in the hush of that sacred moment, Alessia knew...

she didn't just want this.

She was finally ready for all of it.

Chapter 38
Just This

The movie had been on for twenty minutes and neither of them had watched a single scene. Alessia sat curled against Leander's side, her legs tucked beneath her, a bowl of popcorn balanced on the cushion between them. His arm was around her shoulders, his thumb moving in slow absent circles against her skin the way it always did when he wasn't thinking about it. The apartment was warm and dim, just the soft flicker of the television washing blue and gold light across the walls. A half-empty bottle of wine sat on the coffee table beside two glasses, hers closer, his just out of reach because he kept forgetting to drink it.

On screen, someone was running through an airport.

"He's going to miss the flight," Leander said.

"He's not going to miss the flight," Alessia said.

"He never misses the flight."

"How do you know? You've seen this?"

"I haven't seen this. I just know how these things go."

He looked down at her, one brow lifted. "You're one of those people."

"What people?"

"The ones who narrate the movie while it's happening."

She tilted her head up at him. "I prefer to think of it as being ahead of the story."

He laughed, low and easy, and pressed a kiss to her temple. She could feel the smile still on his lips when he did it.

She reached for her wine, took a slow sip, and settled back into him. His shoes were beside the couch where he'd toed them off an hour ago. Hers were still by the door where she'd left them when she arrived, because she always took them off at the door and he was starting to know that about her. The small, quiet things that made her Alessia.

"He missed the flight," Leander said.

She sat up slightly. On screen, the man stood at the gate, watching the plane pull away, his face falling into something devastated and disbelieving.

"Okay," she conceded. "He missed the flight."

"You were saying?"

She threw a piece of popcorn at him.

He caught it. Ate it. Looked insufferably pleased with himself.

She laughed, really laughed. The kind that came from somewhere unguarded, and he pulled her back into him, his chin resting on top of her head. The popcorn bowl shifted between them. Neither moved it. Her hand found his in the dim light and their fingers laced together without either of them deciding to, the way things did between them now. Natural. Unannounced.

Outside, the city hummed its usual low note.

Inside, the candle she'd lit earlier on the kitchen counter had burned down to a soft glow. The wine was almost gone.

They watched the rest of the movie like that.

Not talking much.

Not needing to.

Just the warmth of him, the salt of the popcorn, the man on screen eventually finding his way back to the woman he loved, and the quiet between two people who were starting to understand that this, just this, was its own kind of everything.

Chapter 39

The Longest Touch (Leander's Turn)

The lights were low.

Not dimmed, just lowered by design. Warm amber glowed from a single lamp in the corner, casting soft gold across the sheets. A trio of candles flickered near the nightstand, their flames swaying gently in rhythm with the music.

Alessia lay on her stomach, legs slightly parted just enough to feel unintentional, but still inviting if he wanted her. Her cheek rested on her folded arms. The room was quiet, save for the faint hum of instrumental music and the gentle clink of a bottle cap being twisted open.

The scent hit her first... something earthy and sensual. Almond and vanilla, warm and smooth. He'd chosen well.

Leander's hands hovered above her. She could feel the heat of him, even before he touched her.

Then...

Warm oil.

He rubbed it between his palms, spreading it slowly, deliberately. And then he began at her feet.

He took his time. One foot, then the other. His thumbs circled the pads of her toes, stroked the arch, pressed gently into her heel. She let out a soft sigh she hadn't meant to.

His hands moved up her calves, kneading the muscles in long, sensual strokes. She felt every pass of his thumbs on the inside, and his fingers wrapping around the outside. Slow. Purposeful.

When he reached her thighs, he didn't rush. His fingers moved deliberately along the backs, then the insides. He avoided the place her body silently begged him to reach. Not yet.

The slick glide of his palms slid up her sides. He straddled behind her, his knees on either side, and rubbed oil into her arms next, mirroring the care he'd given her legs. Long strokes, slow squeezes from her wrists to her shoulders.

Each time he leaned forward, she felt him against her… firm, warm, unmistakably there.

She melted beneath him. Her body no longer hers. Just sensation.

Then came her back.

He leaned in, pressing his thumbs deep into the knots along her spine. Found the tension just beneath her shoulder blades and coaxed it out with care. Her breath caught when he dug a little deeper, his fingers strong and sure.

He kissed the base of her neck. "Still with me?" he whispered.

She could only nod.

His hands slid lower. Over the curves of her ass, slick and reverent. He kneaded, pressed, traced. She arched instinctively, a low moan slipping free.

And then, finally, his fingers slipped between her thighs.

Not inside.

Just a tease.

Circling. Stroking. A maddening rhythm that hovered exactly where she needed him, and exactly where he refused to go. The oil made everything feel hotter, smoother. Her body trembled beneath him.

"Leander..." she gasped, hips lifting. "Please."

He slowed. Pressed one finger softly to her entrance, just barely parting her. Then withdrew again with a wicked smile in his voice.

"Not yet," he murmured.

He kissed her spine once more.

"Now," he said, "it's my turn."

Chapter 40

The Longest Touch (Alessia's Turn)

Alessia rose slowly, her body still humming, her breath uneven from all he'd given... and refused to give. She didn't speak. She didn't need to.

Leander moved without question, lying back on the sheets, arms loose at his sides. He didn't close his eyes, but his gaze softened, locked on her with something like reverence.

He wanted to see her.

And she wanted to be seen.

She took the bottle of oil in both hands, let it warm between her palms, then let it drip, one drop at a time, onto the bare skin of his chest. He flinched slightly at first, the sensation unexpected, but then a low sound escaped his throat. Pleasure.

She rubbed her hands together, slow and slick, before placing them gently on his temples.

She started there.

Circles. Light pressure. Just her fingertips smoothing the lines near his hairline. Then his neck. His throat. His collarbones.

She moved lower to his chest... strong and sculpted, but soft under her palms. She lingered there, rubbing oil into his pecs, watching the way his breath shifted beneath her touch. He was already hard. Fully. But she didn't go there yet.

She slid down his arms. Over his shoulders. Across his biceps, his forearms, his wrists. She touched every inch of him with intention... slow, attentive, teasing him not just with her hands, but with her presence.

Then his thighs.

She got close.

Too close.

Each time she passed near his arousal, her knuckles brushed against him... not enough to satisfy, but enough to tease. Enough to make him shift beneath her. Just barely.

Then his calves. His ankles. His feet.

She took her time.

When she was done, she leaned forward and whispered, “Relax. I’ll be right back.”

She turned toward the door, hips swaying, and paused just before reaching it. She looked back.

He hadn’t moved. His eyes were closed now, his arms still at ease, his body glowing with surrender.

Perfect.

She turned silently, padded back to the bed, and climbed on. Then, without a word, she straddled him.

And in one slow, fluid motion, she lowered herself onto him. All the way.

He let out a sigh. Not just from pleasure, but from something deeper. Release. Surrender. Connection.

Her hands braced on his chest as she began to move... slow at first, rising and falling with grace, each inch an exploration. Then she paused. Lifted almost all the way off until only his tip lingered inside her... she played there for a moment, teasing, circling, savoring. Then she sank back down hard enough to make them both gasp.

She leaned forward, her breasts grazing his chest, her weight melting into him. With each thrust, she squeezed around him, tightening just enough to make every motion sharper, fuller. Now, as she rocked back and forth, her clit rubbed against him with every pass... electric, precise, perfect.

Their rhythm shifted.

Built.

Soft became wild.

Stillness became motion.

She kissed his mouth. His jaw. His neck. He gripped her hips, but didn't guide, he didn't need to.

She knew exactly what she was doing.

And when the moment came, when their rhythm broke into something chaotic and real and raw, they cried out together.

He spilled into her as she came undone around him. The sensation of him filling her deep, warm, and overwhelming, sent a final shiver through her entire body.

She loved that feeling.

The fullness.

The connection.

The way it made her feel claimed and safe and completely undone.

One release.

One pulse.

One quiet collapse into something more than pleasure.

She curled into him, her chest rising and falling against his.

He kissed her hair and whispered, “You’re going to ruin me.”

She smiled, still catching her breath.

“Good.”

Chapter 41

What Comes After

Their bodies stilled, breath slowly returning to rhythm. Alessia didn't move, not right away. She lay sprawled across his chest, legs tangled with his, her cheek against the soft rise and fall of his heartbeat.

The room was quiet, golden with the last flickers of candlelight. She could still feel him inside her, the echo of fullness lingering like a memory that refused to fade.

Leander ran his hand down her spine in lazy strokes, his other arm wrapped around her shoulder. Protective. Present.

Neither of them spoke.

Not because there was nothing to say, but because this silence felt full.

Whole.

"Are you okay?" he asked, voice low and rough against her hair.

She nodded, eyes still closed.

"More than okay."

A quiet laugh escaped her.

"What?" he asked.

She tilted her head, smiling against his skin. "I just... I didn't know it could feel like this. So good. So full. So..." She paused. "Safe."

His arm tightened slightly around her. “That’s what it should always feel like.”

She looked up at him, her fingers brushing along the edge of his jaw. “I want to try more things,” she said softly.

His eyes searched hers. “More?”

She nodded. “All the things I used to wonder if I was allowed to want.”

A breath.

“But I want to want them. And I want you to be the one who shows me how.”

His gaze darkened, but there was warmth in it too... reverence, not hunger.

“I’d give you anything,” he said. “You already know that, don’t you?”

Her smile spread wide and slow.

“I’m ready.”

A beat passed.

And then her eyes sparkled with mischief.

Leander’s voice, hoarse with aftershocks:

“What was that move?” he asked.

Alessia (innocent, smug, sensual):

“What move?”

He laughed softly. “Don’t play innocent. The thing you did near the end. That slow rise... the pause... then the mmmm”

He let out a groan, his head falling back against the pillow.

"Whatever that was, it almost killed me."

She laughed softly against him. "Good."

They stayed wrapped in each other for a while longer, her fingers tracing lazy patterns on his chest, his hand still moving softly over her back.

Eventually, Alessia sighed and sat up. "Okay. Shower?"

Leander groaned. "You're not going in there without me."

She slipped out of bed with a teasing glance over her shoulder. "Then come catch me."

He followed.

The bathroom was fogged with steam and soft golden light. The candles they'd forgotten to blow out still burned low. The shower sprayed warm against the glass, the sound hissing softly into the quiet.

Inside, he washed her slowly. His hands over her back, her shoulders, her legs. She leaned into him, water gliding over her skin, eyes half-lidded in peace.

She returned the favor, running soapy hands down his chest, over his thighs, letting her fingers linger in all the places that made him tilt his head back and breathe a little harder.

But they didn't push it.

Not now.

This was about connection. Healing. Trust.

When they stepped out and wrapped themselves in towels, Alessia caught their reflection in the fogged mirror. His body behind hers, both of them flushed and glowing and beautifully undone.

He looked over her shoulder.

“You’re dangerous,” he said quietly.

She met his eyes in the glass.

“And this,” she murmured, “is just the beginning.”

Chapter 42

The Way It Was

The next morning, Alessia stood by the window of Leander's penthouse, wrapped in one of his oversized button-down shirts, a mug of coffee cupped between her palms.

The city stretched out beneath her... confident, loud, alive. But she wasn't thinking about the city. She was thinking about him.

Leander was still asleep in the bedroom behind her, tangled in the sheets they'd ruined with sweat and trust and heat. Her body ached in the best way. Her mind was quiet in a way she hadn't known she craved.

And yet...

That familiar flicker of doubt stirred.

She walked to the small dining table, set down her mug, and pulled out her phone. She didn't open any apps. Just held it. Stared at the screen. Let it reflect back her own thoughts.

Because she had once loved someone who told her she was too much.

Too intense. Too opinionated. Too ambitious. Too open with her emotions. Too sexual, too assertive, too big in all the ways that made her her.

He said those things kindly, at first.

"You feel everything so deeply," he'd murmured once, with a kiss to her temple.

Then later:

"You're exhausting."

Then finally:

"You make it hard to breathe."

So she stopped talking so much. She wore quieter colors. She stayed still when she wanted to dance. She bit her lip when she wanted to scream. She softened herself to stay wanted.

Until she found out he was cheating with someone smaller. Someone safer. Someone easier.

He didn't even deny it.

"You made me feel inadequate," he said. "Like I could never keep up with you."

That version of Alessia, raw, radiant, and unfiltered, had been labeled too much for one man.

So she became less.

Less of herself. More of what she thought people wanted. And when that didn't bring her love, she stopped looking altogether.

Until now.

Until Leander.

She heard him stir in the other room, sheets shifting, a low sigh from the bed.

He made her feel like every version of herself was wanted. The bold one. The quiet one. The one who moaned without shame and the one who cried when she needed to.

She walked back into the bedroom, and he was sitting up now, shirtless, sleepy-eyed, smiling.

"Morning," he said, voice thick with sleep.

She paused in the doorway. "Can I tell you something?"

He nodded instantly. "Always."

She crossed to the bed, climbed in beside him, curling her legs under her.

"I was with someone once who told me I was too much. That I overwhelmed him. That my ambition, my emotions, my... everything was just too big."

Leander's smile faded, replaced by something quieter.

"And for a while," she continued, "I believed him. So I got smaller. I made myself quieter. Softer. Easier to digest."

She looked down at her hands, then up at him. "But with you... I feel like I'm allowed to be everything again."

Leander reached over and tucked a strand of hair behind her ear.

"Don't ever make yourself small for someone else again," he said. "Not even for me."

She laughed, a little teary, a little relieved.

"I'm serious," he added. "You're not too much. You're just enough. For me, you're everything."

He pulled her into his lap, holding her tightly. She melted against him, letting her body rest in the truth of his arms.

In the truth of her.

Chapter 43

Father First

Leander was late.

He didn't mean to be.

But when Adrian called, he always answered.

The mid-morning sun was cutting across the polished glass of his office windows when the call came through. Leander had just texted Alessia a quiet "thinking of you," when Adrian's name lit up his phone.

He answered on the first ring.

"Everything okay?"

A long pause. Then his son's voice, calm but tight.

"Can you come?"

Leander didn't ask for details.

He closed his laptop, grabbed his keys, and left.

⊡

Adrian stood outside the clinic when Leander pulled up... tall, dark-haired, the same strong jaw and quiet fire in his eyes. He was holding a folder, his foot tapping a little too fast against the pavement.

"Is it you?" Leander asked, stepping out of the car.

Adrian shook his head. "No. It's about Mom."

Leander exhaled slowly. "Tell me."

“She’s okay. But her blood pressure was through the roof last night. She wouldn’t let them call me, and by the time they did, she was already being monitored. I came this morning to figure it out.”

“And?”

“She’s stable now. But... Dad, I can’t do this by myself.”

Leander didn’t flinch at the word. Dad.

Adrian rarely used it.

Leander stepped closer, put a hand on his son’s shoulder. “You’re not doing it alone.”

They sat together inside for the next hour. Talking to nurses. Reviewing prescriptions. Discussing options.

Leander didn’t pretend it wasn’t complicated. His relationship with Adrian’s mother had been built on proximity, not passion. The kind of quiet agreement between two people who needed something that wasn’t love. But he never walked away from responsibility.

And Adrian... God, he’d turned into someone incredible.

Focused. Steady. Loyal.

A better man than Leander had been at his age.

By the time they stepped outside again, the afternoon had blurred into evening.

“You’ve got someone waiting for you?” Adrian asked.

Leander paused.

He thought of Alessia.

Of her smile.

Her quiet bravery.

The way she clung to him like he was safe, and the way he felt safer for it.

"I do," he said softly.

Adrian looked sideways at him. "Is she... different?"

Leander gave a quiet smile. "She is."

"Good," Adrian said. "You deserve something real."

Leander clapped a hand on his son's back. "So do you."

⊡

He didn't check his phone until he got back to the car.

There was no message from Alessia.

But a half-written one sat in her name field. She hadn't sent it.

She was waiting.

He smiled and pulled up her contact, thumb flying over the screen.

Leander:

I'm sorry for the silence. Today pulled me into another world for a little while.

I'm back now.

And I can't stop thinking about you.

Tell me where you are, and I'll meet you there. Or tell me nothing and I'll come find you anyway.

Chapter 44

A Quiet Place

Alessia sat barefoot on the drop cloth in the center of her living room.

Her hair was up in a loose twist, wisps falling as she moved. She wore an oversized white tank top spattered with color, no bra underneath, and a pair of black cotton shorts that had seen better days.

Her phone lay on the windowsill behind her… face down.

She hadn't wanted to stare at it.

Not after hours of silence.

Not after everything they'd shared.

She'd typed and deleted a message more than once.

"Hey, just checking in."

"Let me know if you're okay."

"Is this normal for you?"

In the end, she wrote nothing.

Instead, she picked up a brush.

The canvas in front of her wasn't for anyone else. It never had been. Painting was her sanctuary, her quiet. Her clarity. The only time she could stop performing and just… feel.

She moved the brush in long, deliberate sweeps, blending a wash of teal into soft mauve. The colors didn't follow a plan. They never did. She painted emotion, not form. Shadows of longing. Light where there hadn't been any before.

The moment her fingers touched the canvas, her chest loosened.

Here, she wasn't Alessia the boss.

Not the planner.

Not the woman who needed to know where things stood.

She was just color and silence and movement.

And then her phone buzzed.

She let it ring once before she stood, wiped her hands on her thighs, and crossed to the window. A glance at the screen stopped her breath.

Leander.

Her stomach fluttered.

She opened the message slowly, half-bracing for disappointment, half-hoping for everything.

I'm sorry for the silence. Today pulled me into another world for a little while.

I'm back now.

And I can't stop thinking about you.

Tell me where you are, and I'll meet you there. Or tell me nothing and I'll come find you anyway.

Alessia closed her eyes.

She could feel her pulse returning to something soft. Safe.

It was never about being needy, it was about being considered. And he saw her. Always.

She picked up her brush again and dipped it in gold.

Then she sent her reply.

I'm home. Painting. Come find me.

She didn't expect a quick response.

So when the knock came just twenty minutes later, she startled, dropping her brush onto the floor with a soft thud.

She padded barefoot to the door, her tank top streaked with fresh color, the hem of her shorts riding up one thigh. No time to clean up. No time to think.

She opened the door.

There he was.

Leander stood with a single white bag in one hand and something gentle in his eyes.

He took one look at her... barefoot, flushed, paint-smudged, and he smiled like she was art.

"I brought dinner," he said softly.

She stepped aside, heart full.

And as he walked in, she realized she wasn't just being seen.

She was being chosen.

Chapter 45

The Vineyard

They drove through the hills just before sunset.

The windows were down. The warm breeze toyed with Alessia's hair, and Leander reached over more than once just to tuck it behind her ear, his thumb grazing her cheek as if he needed to touch her constantly.

When the estate came into view, Alessia drew in a breath.

It looked like something from a dream. Stone pathways, rows of grapevines stretching out like green ribbons, the golden light settling over everything like honey. Beyond the vineyard, the edge of the villa peeked out. A mix of old-world charm and modern luxury.

"This is yours?" she asked.

"One of them," Leander said, casually. "This one's special, though. I come here when I need to breathe."

She smiled softly. "You brought me to your sanctuary."

He looked at her. "You are my sanctuary."

⊡

They walked slowly between the rows of vines. Alessia's sandals crunched softly on gravel as she brushed her fingers along the leaves. Every few steps, Leander would point something out... Cabernet Sauvignon, Pinot Noir, Chardonnay. Little facts. Quiet stories. A memory from a past harvest or a comment about the soil.

But mostly, he watched her.

She was glowing.

Hair down, skin sun-kissed, wearing a soft linen sundress that clung in all the right places and lifted just slightly in the breeze. She paused to smell a leaf and he felt something in his chest stutter.

“You could be bottled,” he said.

She laughed. “Excuse me?”

“You’re intoxicating.”

She rolled her eyes, but her cheeks flushed.

They came to a clearing where a small wooden table had been set with two wine glasses, a chilled bottle of champagne, and a spread of fruit, cheese, and dark chocolate.

“Leander…” she whispered.

He stepped behind her, arms sliding around her waist.

“I want you to taste everything slowly,” he said into her ear. “Tell me how it feels.”

He poured the champagne and handed her a strawberry. “Eyes closed.”

She obeyed.

The berry touched her lips. Cool. Soft. Juicy.

She bit, and a trickle of juice slipped down her chin.

Leander groaned softly, brushing it away with his thumb and tasting it off his hand. “Perfect.”

He fed her slivers of cheese and sips of wine, guiding her descriptions with quiet questions.

Then came the chocolate... rich and melting against her tongue.

“I want more,” she whispered.

“Oh, I know,” he said.

⊡

The wine cellar was tucked beneath the villa. It was cool, quiet, and dimly lit.

The air smelled like oak and secrets.

Leander led her by the hand between long rows of aging barrels, his voice low. “I’ve thought about having you here.”

She looked up at him, heat blooming low in her belly. “Show me.”

He kissed her there—back against the barrel, his hand sliding up her thigh, pushing the dress higher and higher.

“Do you know what you do to me?” he asked.

“I hope so.”

When his fingers found her, she was already wet.

He pressed her gently forward, one hand on her hip, the other teasing her open.

Then he dropped to his knees.

She gasped when his mouth met her.

Soft licks.

Deep strokes.

His hands on her ass, holding her still as he worshiped every inch of her.

And when she came—hard and fast, clinging to the barrel like it was the only thing tethering her to the earth—he stood, wiped his mouth, and whispered, "My turn."

He turned her gently. Lifted the back of her dress.

His pants were already undone.

She felt him behind her, hard and ready, and braced her hands against the barrel.

The first thrust made her cry out.

The echo of it lingered through the stone walls.

He moved with slow, powerful control—deep, unrelenting. His chest pressed to her back, lips against her ear.

"Anyone could walk in," he murmured.

"I don't care."

"Say it."

She turned her face to meet his gaze. "I don't care."

He groaned, slamming into her harder, his fingers circling her clit until she came again... shaking and pulsing around him.

He came seconds later, spilling into her with a deep, guttural sound that vibrated through her spine.

They stood there for a moment. Their bodies still connected, their breath catching.

Then he pulled her dress down, turned her around, and kissed her like they weren't still tangled in the thrill of being caught.

"Remind me to age wine here more often," she said against his lips.

He smiled. "You're the only thing getting better with time."

Chapter 46

Arrival

The plane dipped low over the coast, skimming the sky with golden light as it began its descent. Alessia leaned toward the window, her breath catching at the first sight of the shoreline.

It looked untouched.

Wide arcs of pale sand cradled by turquoise water, cliffs kissed with ivy and blush-colored blooms, and rooftops made of stone and aged wood, tucked into the lush green like secrets.

Her body tingled. Not from the flight, but from anticipation. From possibility.

When they stepped onto the tarmac, the heat greeted her first. Not oppressive, but inviting. Like silk sliding across her skin. The air was warm and soft, with just a hint of salt and something floral.

She inhaled slowly.

“It smells like gardenia,” she whispered.

Leander looked over at her. “Night-blooming jasmine. It lingers longer in the morning here.”

She smiled. Even that, even that was beautiful.

A sleek car waited for them. Not flashy. Not overdone. Just elegant and quiet, like everything else so far. The drive wasn’t long, but Alessia didn’t rush it. She pressed her fingertips to the window glass, letting herself feel every curve of the road, every rise and dip of the land.

When they arrived, she barely stepped out before two attendants greeted them, not hurried or rehearsed, but warm and deeply present.

“Mr. Moore. Miss...” The woman gave a graceful nod. “Welcome. We’ve been expecting you.”

They were each handed a tall champagne stem. Not filled with champagne, but with something rich and golden, like liquid mango sunlight. Alessia took a sip.

The drink was cool, slightly fizzy, with notes of citrus and vanilla. A hint of ginger warmed the finish.

She turned to Leander, smiling. “That’s not champagne.”

“No,” he said. “Something local. Sweet, bright... unexpected.”

The entrance to the resort was framed by tall palms and brilliant bougainvillea vines, their fuchsia blooms dripping like lace over curved archways. Stone pathways led in winding lines toward the main villa, flanked by massive pots of lavender and citrus trees in bloom.

And then the sound.

Not silence, but layered stillness.

The distant hush of waves curling along the shore. A rustle of leaves in the breeze. The quiet chirp of birds... low and rhythmic. She could even hear the soft clink of glass from somewhere deep within the resort.

Her chest expanded as she breathed it all in.

Peaceful.

But alive.

Inside, the lobby wasn't a lobby at all. It was open-air walls replaced with archways and sheer linen drapes that moved like breath. A grand floral arrangement rested on a stone pedestal in the center, filled with white orchids and wild greenery. Every surface felt hand-touched... worn wood, textured walls, curated art.

A painting caught her eye.

Not quite explicit. But suggestive.

A man's back. A woman's hand slipping around his waist. Their faces turned away, but their intimacy was undeniable.

"Bold," Alessia said quietly, stepping closer to examine the brushstrokes.

Leander stood beside her. "They rotate the art. Local artists. No rules. Just honesty."

She looked at him, surprised. "You designed this?"

He gave a small nod.

She hesitated. "Have you brought women here before?"

He shook his head, his voice quiet but certain. "No. Never. This place isn't for that."

Her eyes searched his, and this time, what she saw there didn't need explaining.

"This is somewhere I love," he added. "And hopefully, it'll be somewhere you love too."

A well-dressed man approached with a warm smile. "Mr. Moore, welcome back."

"Thank you, Mateo," Leander said easily.

Mateo turned to Alessia. “We’re honored to have you here. If there’s anything at all you need, please don’t hesitate to ask.”

Their suite was set on the far edge of the property. Secluded, but still connected by winding garden paths. The building itself was modern but warm... stone, glass, and wood in perfect harmony.

When the door opened, Alessia’s breath caught.

The bed was draped in soft white linen with a canopy of sheer fabric flowing gently above. Bold, abstract artwork lit up the walls... rich color and intimate emotion captured in every brushstroke. A double vanity framed by golden sconces. A curved soaking tub, open to the sky. Floor-to-ceiling glass doors that led out to a private balcony overlooking the ocean.

Two loungers.

A table set for two.

And the sea was endless and calm, stretching into the pale horizon.

“It’s beautiful,” she said, barely above a whisper.

“I want us to feel like we can breathe here,” Leander said softly. “Truly breathe. Let go of everything.”

She walked slowly to the balcony doors and opened them. The breeze hit her instantly... cooler here, touched by the sea. She stepped outside and leaned against the railing.

Below, waves lapped gently against the shore. Farther down, she noticed a tucked-away path winding toward another quiet beach.

A memory rose of another beach. Her bare skin. The feeling of freedom.

This one... might go even further.

She didn't turn around.

"You know," she said, "if you ever want to build another resort... I'd love to help design it."

He stepped behind her, hands sliding around her waist. "You would?"

"I see things differently now," she said. "What space should feel like. What it should invite."

His mouth pressed softly to her shoulder.

"Then we'll build something beautiful," he said. "Together."

She smiled and let the sound of the ocean fill her bones.

This wasn't just another trip.

It was a beginning.

Chapter 47

Tasting Desire

The sky glowed with fading light as Alessia followed the winding path down to the beach. Lanterns flickered along the edges of the walkway... golden flames dancing inside handblown glass.

She heard it before she saw it: the soft, rhythmic hush of waves, the faint clink of glass, the low murmur of music woven with the breeze.

Then she saw the table.

A single setting beneath a canopy of soft white linen, open on all sides to the sea. Pillar candles surrounded the space, their flames swaying gently. The table was draped in deep ivory, the place settings elegant but relaxed. The chairs were low and wide, carved from dark wood and cushioned in cream linen. Between them, a lantern flickered low and warm.

She stepped onto the sand and immediately slipped off her shoes.

The cool, fine grains shifted beneath her toes like silk.

Leander was already there, his back to her as he spoke quietly to a staff member setting down the first course. He turned when he heard her approach.

And smiled.

He looked relaxed... barefoot like her, his shirt unbuttoned halfway down his chest, sleeves casually rolled. As she approached, his eyes traveled the length of her body with no shame, no hunger.

Just appreciation.

"You look..." He paused, stepped closer. "Like the evening was made for you."

She smiled, cheeks warming in the candlelight.

"And you," she said, "look like a man who's finally relaxed."

He took her hand and kissed it, slow. "Sit with me."

She did.

The chair molded around her like a sigh. The breeze touched her bare shoulders. She tipped her head back and closed her eyes for a moment, letting the air, the scent of salt and citrus, the soft heat—all of it—settle into her.

The first course arrived: delicate rolls of marinated melon wrapped in prosciutto, flecked with lime zest and fresh mint.

Beside the plate, a tiny glass filled with pale pink liquid.

"Pairing," Leander explained. "Each course comes with a drink. Just a sip or two. A little sensory game."

She raised a brow. "Who planned this?"

He lifted his own glass. "I did."

She sipped.

Sweet. Sharp. A kiss of something botanical.

"Careful," he added, "some of them are stronger than they taste."

Course after course arrived, small plates with artful precision. Grilled peaches with burrata and black pepper honey. Seared scallops in coconut-lime foam.

A spoonful of mango-laced ceviche resting in a polished shell. Each with its own miniature drink—infusions of herbs, fruit, exotic spirits.

Alessia felt the buzz rising. Not just from the drinks, but from the intimacy.

Every bite.

Every taste.

Every look he gave her.

She leaned closer across the table, one bare foot brushing his ankle. "You planned this to seduce me, didn't you?"

He didn't deny it.

"Maybe I planned dessert to seduce you."

She laughed, and he stood.

"Come with me."

He led her a few feet away to a lounge cushion laid directly in the sand. A small table sat beside it, and on it, a domed silver tray, covered.

He motioned for her to sit.

She did.

He lifted the lid.

Alessia blinked.

It wasn't just dessert.

It was... art.

Fresh strawberries sliced thin and shaped into a blooming flower. A long curl of dark chocolate, resting across a bed of whipped vanilla bean mousse. A small glass pot of thick golden honey. And beside it, a silver spoon.

Her eyes met his.

"That's not dessert," she murmured.

"It's inspiration," he said softly.

He reached for the strawberry, dipped its edge in the mousse, then into the honey. Brought it to her lips.

"Open."

She did.

The flavors exploded... sweet, smooth, just the edge of bitterness from the dark chocolate that followed. His fingers brushed her lips as he withdrew.

She moaned softly, licking a drop of honey from the corner of her mouth.

He watched.

Heat flickered in his eyes.

Then he dipped two fingers in the mousse and smeared it lightly across her collarbone.

Her breath caught.

He leaned in and licked it off.

Slow.

Precise.

"Leander..."

He dipped the spoon into the honey next.

"I thought," he murmured, "maybe you'd like to play with dessert too."

He handed her the spoon. Sat back. Open. Waiting.

The candles flickered brighter in the wind.

And Alessia smiled... wicked, alive, and completely herself.

She took the spoon.

And chose where to begin.

Chapter 48

Tasting You

The silver spoon in Alessia's hand felt heavier than it should.

Not because of weight, but because of promise.

She dipped it into the pot of honey slowly, watching the amber ribbon slide and curl around the edge. It caught the candlelight as it dripped, thick and golden.

Leander sat back on the cushion, his shirt fully unbuttoned now, his chest bare and golden in the flickering glow. He watched her with a hunger that didn't rush.

No commands.

No pressure.

Just permission.

Invitation.

Alessia leaned forward and let one drop fall onto his chest, just above his heart.

His breath hitched.

She followed it with her tongue.

The taste was richer on him. Warmer. She lingered, lips brushing his skin, then kissed the same spot softly before pulling back.

He exhaled through his nose, eyes never leaving hers.

"I could get used to dessert like this," he murmured.

She dipped the spoon again, this time trailing a fine line of honey along the edge of his collarbone. Then lower, toward the ridge of his abs.

She followed every inch with her mouth... soft kisses, light licks, and warm breath.

He was already hard beneath his linen pants. And she hadn't even touched him there.

Yet.

She set the spoon aside and picked up a strawberry. Dipped it into the whipped mousse, then leaned over him.

"Open," she said, echoing his earlier command.

He obeyed.

She fed it to him slowly, watching the way his lips closed around her fingers. Watching the way he sucked the mousse from her skin with a low groan that made her knees press together.

She reached for the chocolate curl next. Broke off a small piece and placed it between her lips.

Then leaned in and kissed him. Letting the dark sweetness melt between them.

The kiss deepened. Grew. His hands came to her hips, pulling her closer, until she was straddling him fully. The thin fabric of her dress bunched at her thighs, her body bare beneath.

She pressed against him. Slowly rocked. And he groaned again, deep this time. Needy.

She pulled back just enough to whisper, "Your turn."

His brows lifted. "My turn to eat?"

"No," she said, picking up the pot of honey again. "Your turn to be the plate."

He watched her, smiling and totally still, as she dipped her fingers into the mousse and dragged them across her chest. Across one breast, then the other. Her nipples hardened instantly in the air.

Then the honey.

She let it trail down the curve of her stomach. Lower. Just above her core.

He cursed under his breath, sitting up straighter.

"Tell me what to do," he rasped.

She smiled, wicked and soft all at once.

"Lick," she said. "All of it."

He didn't need to be told twice.

He started at her chest, his tongue slow and lips reverent. He sucked each nipple into his mouth, gentle then firm, swirling, tasting, devouring.

She arched back with a moan.

Then he followed the honey trail... licking along her ribs, down her belly, until he reached the place just above her sex.

He paused. Looked up at her.

"Everything?" he asked, voice rough with restraint.

She nodded.

And he lowered his head.

She cried out at the first touch of his tongue. The mixture of honey and heat and need was almost too much. He licked slowly at first, then circled, then flicked. His fingers came up to part her gently, letting him taste all of her.

She bucked against him. Moaned his name.

When her legs started to tremble, he wrapped an arm around her thighs and pulled her closer, deeper, his mouth working her like a prayer.

And when she came, it was full-bodied. Loud. Her fingers tangled in his hair, her whole body writhing beneath the pressure of his tongue.

He didn't stop until her moans turned to gasps, until her body started to pull away from overstimulation.

Then, only then, did he lift his head.

His mouth glistened. His breath was heavy. And his eyes were wild with love.

"You taste better than dessert," he said.

She laughed, pulling him up, letting him hover above her.

"What now?" he asked.

She kissed him deeply, messy, and tasting herself on his lips.

And whispered against his mouth, "Now we rest. Because tomorrow... I want more."

Chapter 49

The Wild Path

The helmets were matte black. Sleek. A little intimidating.

Alessia ran her fingers along the edge of hers and looked at the ATV... powerful, mud-splattered, and humming with quiet promise.

"You sure you're ready for this?" Leander asked, strapping on his gloves with a grin.

She smirked. "Try to keep up."

He laughed, low and rich, and climbed onto his ATV like he'd done it a thousand times.

The sun was just starting its climb, golden light filtering through dense leaves. The jungle air was thick and green, bursting with life. Wildflowers clung to vines. Everything smelled of earth and citrus.

The guide gave them a few instructions, then waved them forward.

And then they were off.

The engines roared to life beneath them, and Alessia's laughter soared louder than the trail behind her. They twisted through turns and flew down dips, dodging branches, splashing through shallow streams. Her hair blew free, her cheeks flushed with exhilaration. She looked back to see Leander catching up, mud on his shirt, joy in his eyes.

They raced. They teased.

They were absolutely, undeniably alive.

When the trees broke and sunlight poured through, she gasped.

Before them: a hidden waterfall.

Tucked between moss-covered cliffs and tall swaying palms, it shimmered in golden light. A natural pool rippled below it, clear and cool and untouched.

She pulled off her helmet, heart still pounding, and looked at Leander. "This looks like something from a dream."

He didn't answer.

He was looking at her.

She felt her cheeks flush. Not from exertion this time.

They stripped out of muddy shirts and boots and stepped barefoot onto the warm stones.

The water was brisk... sharp at first, then soothing. It wrapped around her thighs like silk. Leander stepped deeper, then held out a hand to her. She reached for it, and he pulled her into the pool.

They stood chest-deep, mist curling around them, the roar of the falls behind them and nothing but breath between them.

Her hands found his shoulders. His fingers grazed her waist.

The quiet was electric.

Then, as if it had been waiting for this exact moment, he leaned in, kissed her softly once, and whispered–

"I love you."

She blinked, stunned. Her heart tripped in her chest.

"What?"

He didn't back away.

"I love you," he repeated. "Since the moment you stopped hiding. Maybe even before that."

She stared at him. The man who had touched every part of her—body, mind, soul—and never once asked her to be less.

She swallowed hard. "You beat me to it."

He smiled. "That's the only race I plan on winning."

A laugh broke from her lips. And then she kissed him.

Longer this time. Deeper. Her hands slid around his neck, her body pressing against his in the water.

She pulled back just far enough to say, "I love you too."

He pressed his forehead to hers, both of them breathing heavy but not from the ride.

From this.

From truth.

From everything that was changing.

As the waterfall crashed behind them and mist wrapped around their bare shoulders, he wrapped his arms around her back and she lifted her legs to straddle him. He didn't rush it. They didn't need to. They just floated there together, soaked in something neither of them had expected, but both of them now knew.

This wasn't just lust.

This was the beginning of love.

Chapter 50

The Spa and the Spark

The robe slid from her shoulders like it had been waiting for her to stop holding on.

Warm hands welcomed her as she stepped into the candlelit room. One masseuse at her shoulders, another at her feet. Alessia lay down on the heated table, the air thick with the scent of lavender and sea salt, and let her breath go.

Not just an exhale.

A release.

Every knot they touched was one she didn't realize she'd been carrying: between her shoulder blades, beneath her ribs, along the small curve of her spine. With each slow press, her body remembered what it was to be cared for without needing to earn it.

She didn't speak.

Didn't need to.

The music was soft—harp strings, maybe, or some distant wind instrument—and her thoughts drifted somewhere warm, somewhere without fear. She felt her limbs melt into the table, felt herself soften under the pressure.

For the first time in a long time, she let someone else do the holding.

When the massage was over, her robe was returned... fresh, soft, and infused with jasmine. Her feet slid into slippers that felt like clouds, and she was led down a quiet hallway toward the spa garden. Fountains bubbled gently. The air was thick with mist and orchids. She turned a corner and saw him.

Leander.

Leaning casually against a stone column, glass of something amber in his hand.

His gaze swept over her slowly. Not lustful.

Adoring.

“You,” he said, “are glowing.”

She smiled, a little dizzy from the quiet, the warmth, and him.

“I think I finally stopped thinking.”

“Good,” he said. “Then let’s not think a moment longer.”

He offered her a hand and led her to a low, candlelit table nestled beneath a flowering tree. A bottle sat between two glasses. Not wine. Something sparkling. Bright.

“What is this?” she asked.

He poured. “Local. Sweet. Made with herbs I can’t pronounce. You’ll like it.”

She took a sip. And laughed.

He watched her like she was a gift. And in that moment, Alessia didn’t feel the need to be impressive or clever or beautiful.

She just was.

And that was enough.

They didn't rush. They sat beneath the tree until the sky darkened and stars blinked awake. They talked softly about music, about memories, and about things they'd never told anyone.

Eventually, he reached across the table and traced the inside of her wrist.

"I've never seen you more relaxed," he said.

"That's because I finally feel safe."

He turned her palm over and kissed it, slow and sure.

"And that," he whispered, "is the sexiest thing I've ever seen."

Chapter 51

A Place Without Shame

The sand was cooler now.

Silken beneath her feet, it curled between her toes as she walked, the waves whispering just beside her.

Alessia was completely naked.

And not just in body, but in spirit.

No swimsuit to shield her. No towel clutched around her hips. Just the warm evening air brushing her skin, the salt tang of the ocean, and the man walking beside her.

Leander.

They strolled quietly, letting the hush of the waves and the occasional murmur of distant voices fill the space between them. The nude beach stretched out along the coast, soft golden lanterns flickering every few feet, casting just enough light to blur outlines but not enough to hide.

She saw other couples.

Some walking. Some curled up on towels, lost in their own world. Some talking quietly, some laughing.

No one stared.

No one judged.

And that was the magic.

It didn't feel obscene.

It felt... open.

As they neared the edge of the lit path, she saw it. A canopy bed, tucked into the dune's curve. The frame was wood, aged and soft to the touch. Sheer curtains draped down in gauzy ripples, fluttering in the breeze like whispers.

At its center: a pale linen blanket, folded, waiting.

He looked at her. "Here?"

She didn't answer.

She stepped forward first.

Leander followed, and together they unfolded the blanket, smoothing it over the cushion of the cabana bed. The fabric was cool, but Alessia was warm, from the inside out.

They climbed in.

The curtain swayed closed behind them, offering just enough privacy to soften the scene, but not enough to separate them from the world.

They lay on their sides at first... face to face, close, but not touching.

His gaze searched hers.

No one spoke.

And then her hand moved first.

She slid it down his chest, letting her fingers trail over the muscle, the soft hair, the smooth plane of his stomach. He sucked in a breath, already responding to her touch.

She leaned in and kissed his collarbone.

Not his mouth.

Not yet.

He touched her next.

A soft stroke down her side, the back of his hand brushing her hip. Then her thigh. Then back up, curling lightly beneath her breast, teasing her nipple into a tight peak.

She gasped softly, the sound lost in the hush of the sea breeze.

A flicker of movement beyond the curtain caught her eye.

A couple walking past.

She could hear them laughing softly now, their voices low.

And something inside her, something old and afraid, began to rise.

But Leander caught her gaze and held it.

"You're safe," he whispered.

And she believed him.

She leaned into his touch.

And then she said, "Don't stop."

His eyes darkened.

He kissed her. Deeply. Fully. His hand moved lower, sliding between her legs, finding her already wet, already trembling.

She opened for him.

And the world... didn't stop.

The couple walked on. Another soft voice drifted past the canopy.

No one lingered. No one watched.

But the possibility of it was enough to make her body arch into his hand.

He pulled back just slightly. "Alessia..."

She silenced him with her lips.

Then whispered against his mouth, "Right here. I want you."

She climbed on top of him, their bodies aligning effortlessly, skin to skin, pulse to pulse. He gripped her hips and she sank onto him with a moan that got lost in the waves.

Slowly, she began to move.

The curtains shifted. The night air kissed her back.

And as they rocked together, completely bare to the night, her body trembling from the buildup and the thrill and the knowing, she realized something:

This wasn't about being seen.

This was about not hiding.

This was her body.

Her desire.

Her choice.

They moved together in a rhythm that had nothing to do with performance and everything to do with presence. He touched her like he was memorizing her. She rode him like she was claiming him.

And when they both came, it was quiet and powerful. Her forehead pressed to his. Their breath tangled. Their hands clenched.

After, they stayed there.

Still connected.

Still exposed.

Still whole.

Leander cradled her gently, one hand splayed across her back, the other brushing loose strands of hair from her cheek. Alessia lay quiet against his chest, her legs still tangled with his, the rhythm of his breath grounding her.

And then, without warning...

A single tear slipped down her cheek.

Not from sadness.

Not even from joy.

But from something deeper, a quiet recognition. A letting go. A becoming.

He felt it.

He didn't ask why.

He only tightened his arm around her, pressing a kiss to the crown of her head.

She didn't wipe the tear away.

Because in that moment, naked in every sense of the word, she felt like herself for the first time.

Seen.

Held.

Safe.

And trusted.

Not just with her body, but with her truth.

She closed her eyes, whispered against his chest, “Thank you.”

And he knew.

It wasn’t for the sex.

It wasn’t for the pleasure or even the freedom.

It was for something far more sacred.

For seeing her.

For not flinching when she unraveled.

For holding every part of her—every contradiction, every fear, every edge—with reverence instead of restraint.

He pressed another kiss to her temple, his voice a low hum against her skin.

“You’re safe with me.”

And she was.

The tide whispered on.

And in the hush of that sacred moment, Alessia knew—

she didn’t just want this.

She had always belonged to it.

She was finally home.

Chapter 52

The Morning After Everything

The sun rose slowly, like it, too, wanted to linger in that moment.

Alessia stirred as its golden light slipped through the white linen of the balcony curtains. Casting long shadows across the floor and onto the bed where she lay naked and still tangled in Leander's arms.

For a long moment, she didn't move.

She just breathed.

The scent of salt lingered in the air. Her muscles ached in the most satisfying way. Her heart... was quiet.

Not racing.

Not hiding.

Just steady.

She turned slightly and looked at him.

Leander lay beside her, still asleep, one hand curled against her stomach, his chest rising and falling in even rhythm. The morning light gilded the edges of his jaw, softened the angles of his mouth. She watched him like one watches a flame... entranced, not wanting to blink.

And for the first time in as long as she could remember...

She didn't feel like she needed to run.

She reached for his hand and brought it to her lips. He stirred, eyes still closed, and pulled her gently closer.

“Mmm,” he murmured. “Is the sun up?”

“Barely,” she whispered. “But I’m not ready to leave yet.”

His arms tightened. “Then we don’t have to.”

But they did.

They both knew it.

Still, they took their time.

A slow shower. A shared cup of coffee out on the balcony, both of them wrapped in robes and watching the horizon turn from gold to blue. The resort below was beginning to wake. Servers moved quietly between tables. Birds called from the canopy of flowering trees. The ocean lapped gently at the shore, calm and rhythmic.

Everything felt slower here.

More deliberate.

And maybe that’s what she’d miss most.

Not just the luxury.

But the permission to pause.

As they packed, she took one last long look around the suite. The open windows, the canopy bed, the drift of white curtains, the champagne glasses still on the table from the night before.

She didn’t feel sadness.

She felt gratitude.

And, if she was honest, excitement.

Leander noticed her pause and came to stand behind her. "We'll come back," he said quietly, his arms sliding around her waist.

She smiled. "I'd like that."

He kissed her cheek. "There's a whole world I want to show you, Alessia."

She turned in his arms. "Where would we go next?"

He tilted his head thoughtfully. "Maybe a vineyard in Tuscany. Or a long weekend in Rome. Or Ireland in the fall... I want you to see places that make you feel alive just by standing still."

She leaned into him. "You've already shown me that. But I want more."

He smiled. "Good. Because there's more. There's always more with you."

They didn't rush their goodbye. The staff saw them off with polite bows and knowing smiles. A car waited with chilled water and soft music. Alessia slipped off her sandals as she climbed in, letting her bare feet press into the floor.

As the resort disappeared behind them, she felt something shift... not fall away, but unfold.

She wasn't leaving something behind.

She was taking it with her.

All of it.

And though the next chapter hadn't been written yet...

She already knew the story was far from over.

Epilogue

The Ring

Leander sat on the balcony as the morning rose behind him, soft and golden. The air was quiet but alive... waves curling below, a distant gull crying once, the whisper of her movement inside.

She didn't know he was watching.

Didn't know how she looked just then. Barefoot, hair loose and shining, wrapped in one of his shirts like she belonged in it. Not because it fit, but because she made everything hers.

He smiled.

She was radiant without trying. Not just in body, but in mind. In presence.

She thought too deeply, felt too much, questioned everything. She challenged him, softened him, turned silence into comfort and heat into clarity.

God, she was beautiful.

Not in the way people described women when they didn't know what else to say.

She was beautiful in the way fire was beautiful... undeniable. Fierce and alive and impossible to look away from. She felt deeply. Thought sharply. Moved through the world with a kind of grace that came from knowing exactly how hard it had tried to break her.

He reached into his bag and opened the box without ceremony.

The ring sat inside.

Simple. Stunning. Hers.

He'd chosen it without hesitation. Not because it sparkled, but because it didn't need to shout to be seen. Like her, it drew attention by simply existing.

He didn't picture the proposal.

Didn't rehearse it. Didn't stage it in his mind.

What mattered was the knowing.

That he wanted her brilliance beside him. Her hunger for life, her boldness, her softness, her spark.

He wanted to build a world around her fire, not dim it.

He closed the box and set it gently back in his bag.

Not today.

But soon.

And when the moment came, he wouldn't need a script.

He'd just need her.

www.ingramcontent.com/pod-product-compliance
Lightning Source LLC
LaVergne TN
LVHW010917110826
845149LV00013B/2391

* 9 7 8 1 9 6 9 0 9 7 2 9 4 *